Kasey Michaels

TO MARRY AT
Christmas

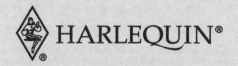

HARLEQUIN®

TORONTO • NEW YORK • LONDON
AMSTERDAM • PARIS • SYDNEY • HAMBURG
STOCKHOLM • ATHENS • TOKYO • MILAN • MADRID
PRAGUE • WARSAW • BUDAPEST • AUCKLAND

ISBN 0-373-81127-6

TO MARRY AT CHRISTMAS

Copyright © 1988 by Kasey Michaels.

All rights reserved. Except for use in any review, the reproduction or
utilization of this work in whole or in part in any form by any electronic,
mechanical or other means, now known or hereafter invented, including
xerography, photocopying and recording, or in any information storage
or retrieval system, is forbidden without the written permission of the
publisher, Harlequin Enterprises Limited, 225 Duncan Mill Road,
Don Mills, Ontario, Canada M3B 3K9.

All characters in this book have no existence outside the imagination of
the author and have no relation whatsoever to anyone bearing the same
name or names. They are not even distantly inspired by any individual
known or unknown to the author, and all incidents are pure invention.

This edition published by arrangement with Harlequin Books S.A.

® and TM are trademarks of the publisher. Trademarks indicated with
® are registered in the United States Patent and Trademark Office, the
Canadian Trade Marks Office and in other countries.

www.eHarlequin.com

Printed in U.S.A.

Chapter One

Elizabeth Chatham moved the small cardboard Sale sign precisely one and one-half inches to the left, then stood back to admire her handiwork. "There," she said, tilting her head to one side and narrowing her eyes to inspect the display of food processors. "That's perfect, Judy, a real work of art. Just let Mr. Lancaster try to find something wrong with it this time!"

"I didn't say he didn't like it, Ms. Chatham," the chubby redhead put in, pushing herself away from the counter that she had been leaning against just as the bell sounded over the loudspeaker, alerting the employees that it was ten o'clock and Lancaster's Department Store was open for business.

"I just said he looked at it sort of funny when he walked by it Saturday while you were on your lunch break."

Elizabeth wrinkled up her small nose in distaste. "And, according to you, that funny look is known as the kiss of death around here. Right, Judy? I've only been here a week, but I've heard enough stories about our esteemed boss to figure out he's a perfectionist. No matter who's responsible, he holds the head buyers guilty as charged for everything and anything that goes wrong within a department. And to think I believed life would be easier here than at my last job."

Judy Holland, who was still in awe knowing her new supervisor had worked at the famous Bloomingdale's department store—in New York City, no less—looked admiringly at Elizabeth's fashionable mauve cable-knit sweater and soft wool plaid skirt and gushed, "Bloomie's! How could you ever bear to leave all that to come back to dinky Bethlehem, Pennsylvania? I'd die to work there!"

"It wasn't all that glamorous, Judy," Elizabeth told the young salesclerk while walking around the counter to check the display from another angle. "Housewares are housewares and bosses, unfortunately, are bosses. Besides, I happen to think that Bethlehem is beautiful. All our lovely old Moravian homes and everything, you know."

As Judy went off to help a woman who was intent on dismantling the blow-dryer display—in an effort to uncover a "pink one to match my bathroom, you understand"—Elizabeth walked through the large third-floor department, giving it one last inspection before heading for her office and the mountain of correspondence waiting for her there. Although she was stationed in the main store, she was housewares buyer for all thirty-six Lancaster department stores that were spread up and down the East Coast, and that meant a lot of paperwork.

She was happy in Bethlehem, she thought comfortably, smiling to herself as she hung a wire whisk back on its hook. Life was less hectic here, with not nearly as much hustle and bustle as in Manhattan, and she definitely didn't miss rush hour on the subway. Her family's huge three-story Victorian home was only a mile from Lancaster's, on quiet, tree-lined Spring Street, and she enjoyed the walk to and from work under the lovely old Hill to Hill Bridge.

Elizabeth was a small-town girl at heart, having grown up the eldest of four children in a loving, middle-class family. Besides, it wasn't as if she had left the love of her life behind her in New York. During her three years at Bloomingdale's she had rarely dated, and she knew firsthand that a person could live a long time in New York City and—although she had made many friends—still feel very much alone.

Pulling a wry face at these thoughts, she knew her grandmother's pointed comments the night before—it was her contention that Elizabeth must be the only unmarried, unsettled twenty-six-year-old female left in civilization—had a lot to do with her current introspection; she stopped in front of a display of cookware and shook her head.

"I'll never understand it," she groused, once again a demanding buyer, picking up the hammered metal roasting pan with some effort and turning back the way she had come. "This thing weighs a ton!"

Rushing a bit in her eagerness to get back to her office and dash off a nasty note to the jobber who had shipped the pan, Elizabeth rounded the corner of the next counter sharply—and ran smack into a tall, immovable object.

"What the—" Nicholas Lancaster had known there was a new head buyer in the housewares division of Lancaster's Downtown but, as Chief Operating Officer, he had never felt any pressing need to immediately introduce himself to every new employee.

His usual method was much more subtle, even sneaky: strolling into the department unannounced within a few days of the latest hiring to observe his newest employee firsthand before making his identity known. This morning had seemed like a good time to observe Ms. Elizabeth Chatham. Although the staff eventually recognized their boss, the initial element of surprise had served him well over the years, and he prided himself on keeping his employees hopping.

But this morning the tables were turned, and it was Nick who was suddenly hopping because his newest employee had come barreling around the towering aisle-display of toasters, which he was inspecting, and violently crashed into him, the roasting pan she was carrying dropping squarely on his foot.

"Oooh!" Elizabeth exclaimed, her breath partially knocked out of her by the force of the impact, while Nick cursed silently, knowing there had to be better ways to meet his new employees. By reading her name tag, he realized at once that the woman was the new buyer, a random conclusion that flitted swiftly through his mind, just a second before the jarring pain in his foot completely registered in his brain.

After the shock of the initial impact was over they both stared blankly at each other for a moment, mumbled startled apologies, then bent down to retrieve the pan, only to bump heads and apologize again, bend down again, and bump heads a second time.

Nick and Elizabeth both ended up sitting rump down in the carpeted aisle, she still furiously apologizing and offering to send for the store nurse, and he, suddenly, inexplicably breathless, holding his injured foot and surreptitiously waving away the three apprehensive salesclerks who were hastening to assist their boss.

"Oh, I'm *so* sorry, sir!" Elizabeth repeated earnestly, one hand to her mouth, knowing deep in her heart that the man she had barreled into could be none other than her boss. Who else could it be, what with her legendary poor timing? Lordy, how she hated Mondays! And why was he staring at her like that?

"Yes, I believe you've already covered that," Nick replied absently, flexing his injured foot and deciding that two things in this department had to go—the high display, and the heavy pan. Then he stole another look at Elizabeth and blinked hard. *She's gorgeous!*

"I know I must sound like a broken record, but then what else can I say? Are you sure you're really all right?" Elizabeth continued breathlessly as she knelt forward to quickly unlace his shoe and massage his stockinged foot, her chestnut head bent over her task and hopefully hiding her flushed cheeks.

Nick leaned back on his hands, doubting what he was seeing, what he was feeling. He felt as if someone had punched him in the stomach, as if he should be gasping to regain his breath, and his heart was pounding at twice its normal rate. He felt like Christmas and the Fourth of July and his birthday had somehow all come at once, without warning, and he had just been given every gift he'd ever wanted. "You—you don't have to do that, you know," he felt honor bound to say, secretly hoping she'd never stop.

It was silly—something she'd only read about in novels—but when her hand made contact with his foot, a tingle moved through Elizabeth's fingers and up her arm. A few seconds later, their gazes met, and held, and the tingle spread throughout her body, warming her blood and turning her bones to water.

"It must hurt terribly, I'm sure. Isn't that just the stupidest pan you ever saw? I was taking it to the stockroom just so something like this wouldn't happen. Arnold Schwarzenegger would have trouble with that thing. I mean, really! Can you imagine a housewife trying to lift that pan with a fifteen-pound turkey in it?" *That's it, Elizabeth,* she congratulated herself. *Keep talking, just keep talk-*

ing. Maybe then he won't notice that you're eyeing him as if you're a starving fool and he's a juicy porterhouse steak. Lordy, but he's gorgeous! So dark, so handsome!

"I can't imagine," Nick murmured, still feeling somewhat bemused. *Her hair wasn't red—sort of burnished brown, maybe? It looks warm. Perhaps if I touched it—*

"I'm sending all of them straight back to the supplier, of course. I can't help but wonder what the previous buyer could have been thinking of when he ordered the things, can you?" *Why is he staring at me like that? Chatham, for pity's sake— enough, already—close your mouth!*

"Maybe, with all this carrying on about physical fitness and incidental exercise, he was hoping to add his bit to the effort?" *Oh, that's good, Lancaster. Ha, ha. Good grief, what a stupid, stuffed-shirt thing to say!*

Elizabeth tilted her head to one side as she considered what he had said, wondering why she thought each word to be a pearl of the greatest wisdom. "Do you really think so? And here I was, imagining the designer as a woman hater, doing his darndest to kill us all off come Thanksgiving. I guess I won't enclose a nasty note after all. There," she ended, giving his foot a final rub, hating to break this small physical contact. "I don't think anything's broken, and my offer still stands to send for the store nurse. I really am sorry about this.''

Nick watched as Elizabeth deftly replaced his shoe and then neatly tied it, giving the finished bow a quick pat as if to put her personal seal of approval on the job. He was desolate with disappointment now that her touch had been withdrawn, but tried not to let it show. ''Is that it? My mother used to kiss my boo-boos to make them all better,'' he teased provocatively as he helped the new buyer to her feet. *That's even worse than your last jewel, Lancaster. Now you sound like a cheap pickup artist trying out the same old tired line. What's the matter with you?*

''She did, did she? How nice for you.'' Pushing a hand through her hair in order to rearrange it behind her ears, Elizabeth looked up at him and smiled, unknowingly sending another stunning blow straight to Nick's midsection as she decided his eyes somehow managed to be both blue and green at the same time.

Nick returned her smile, unsurprised to find himself wondering if all their children would have such beautiful, clear skin. ''Yes, she did. And then she put a bandage on it, whether it needed it or not.''

''You were a very lucky child,'' Elizabeth told

him as he bent down to pick up the roasting pan and place it on a nearby countertop, barely suppressing her desire to lean down herself and run her fingers through his thick, dark hair. "I was always told to stop sniffling, blow my nose and run out to play like a good girl."

Nick felt a sudden, mad urge to take Elizabeth in his arms and kiss her from head to toe to make up for any time she had cried and been denied comfort.

"I'm sorry," he heard himself say inanely, holding on to the countertop because he felt in danger of falling into the velvet soft depths of her wide brown eyes. Her lips would taste like sugary cotton candy, he was sure of it, and he had to hold himself back before he took her in his arms right in the middle of the sales floor. He shook his head slowly, wondering when it was that he had lost his mind. *I've heard about love at first sight, but this is ridiculous!*

"There now," Elizabeth said, pushing the roasting pan away from the edge of the countertop, deciding it might be safest if she pretended she didn't know who he was. "If you think you can trust me not to assault you with a pastry brush or something, perhaps you can tell me how I may help you. I'm Elizabeth Chatham, by the way, and although I'm fairly new here, I believe I can be of assistance. What will it be? A four-slice toaster? A microwave? Or how about a gourmet frying pan?''

''How about lunch, Ms. Chatham? You see, I'm not a customer. I'm Nicholas Lancaster, and your boss,'' Nick replied, forgetting that it was only a few minutes past ten, and the store had just opened.

Elizabeth tilted her head to one side, the single dimple in her left cheek making a startling appearance as she looked up into his face, and with her answer made Nicholas Lancaster the happiest man on the face of the earth. ''Thank goodness!'' she said frankly, feeling her heart skip yet another beat. ''I thought you'd never ask.''

''Liz, pass the potatoes, wouldya? Liz? *Liz!* Hey, *Lizzie*, I want the spuds!''

Elizabeth shook her head, as if waking from a dream, and looked across the dinner table at her brother. ''I'm sorry. Did you say something, Johnny?''

''Oh, brother!'' Fourteen-year-old Paul rolled his eyes and nudged John with his elbow. ''Liz looks like Meggie when she's mooning over some creep. You know—stupid.''

''You always look stupid, *Paulie*,'' Megan, who had just turned seventeen and was totally disenchanted with younger men—especially younger brothers—shot back, her voice spanning two octaves.

"All right, children. That will be quite enough, thank you." The three youngest Chatham children were immediately reduced to glaring at one another in silence. Gloria Chatham, resuming her seat at the foot of the table after bringing in a fresh loaf of bread from the kitchen, shook her head and complained to her husband, "Jack, can't you keep these children from open warfare for two minutes?"

Smiling at his wife, Jack Chatham then turned and winked at his mother, who sat to his right at the other end of the long table, before answering. "Nope. One minute is about thirty seconds over my limit. Besides, I can bellow all day long and they just keep right on talking. You're doing a great job, hon. You just tell them to stop and they stop. I don't know how you do it, and I'm not going to go upsetting the applecart now by trying to take your job away from you. Right, Mom?"

"Don't look at me, son. For myself, I'd like to send them all to reform school, nasty little beggars."

Megan giggled, then leaned over to give her grandmother a kiss on the cheek. "Oh, Gammy, you're such a monster. Last week you wanted us all to sign up with the Foreign Legion. You even rented *Beau Geste* for the VCR.''

''Yes, well,'' the woman muttered, shifting in her seat, ''I figured it was worth a shot. You can't blame an old lady for trying.''

''Gammy, you're adorable! Old lady, indeed. You'll never be old; not if you live to be a thousand.'' Elizabeth leaned back in her chair and lovingly cast her gaze around the table. ''You may all think I should be locked up for saying this but, gosh, am I glad to be home. Unbelievable as it seems, I really missed this madhouse when I was living in New York.''

Rose Chatham, her petite blond beauty only slightly faded with age, blushed at her oldest granddaughter's backhanded compliment, then declared, ''You're pretty adorable yourself, sweetheart. Now pass John the potatoes before he climbs across the table on all fours to get them himself. My stars, child, you were a million miles away a minute ago. You meet your Mr. Right today or something?''

Seeing her oldest daughter's obvious embarrassment at her mother-in-law's blunt question, Gloria broke in hurriedly. ''Elizabeth, is that a new sweater? I particularly like the color; it looks lovely on you.''

''This old thing? Why, no, I—''

"Of course it looks lovely," Rose interrupted, "it matches her flaming cheeks. You don't really think you can hide anything from your old Gammy now do you, child? Come on, what's his name? Did you meet him at work or did he try to pick you up on your walk home? I told you that you should take my car. I hardly ever use it anymore, and the bus stops at the corner if I really want to go anywhere all that badly. I ride half fare, you know, now that I'm an official old lady. Is he handsome, or are you just feeling desperate after our little talk last night? Well, don't just sit there, child—talk to me!"

"I think Elizabeth's waiting for you to take a breath, Mom, so that she can get a word in edgewise," Jack suggested, earning himself a speaking look from his parent. "Uh—right. I'll stay out of it. John, save some of those potatoes in case somebody else wants a second helping. I know the coach told you to bulk up, but you don't have to do it all in one sitting."

Shoveling one last heaping spoonful onto his plate, John passed the bowl over to his father. "Coach says I need more upper-body strength for basketball. I have to build up my muscles. Here you go, Dad. Hey, can't you see Liz going to work in Gammy's car? What a riot!"

Megan leaned over to whisper to Elizabeth. "If

you ask me, Johnny's got plenty of upper-body muscle already—and it's all right between his overgrown ears.''

Paul, not hearing his sister's remark, quickly contradicted his brother, saying, ''I don't know if that would be so bad. One look at that old heap of Gammy's and her boss would give her a raise right on the spot, just so she wouldn't leave that wreck in his parking lot anymore.''

''If you've all quite finished?'' Rose interjected dryly before clearing her throat and commanding: ''Megan, I think your mother needs some help with the dishes. Boys, take a hike before I change my mind about driving you over to Eddie's this Saturday. Jack, go read your paper in the living room. Elizabeth Anne—*sit!*''

Elizabeth, who had risen along with her mother and was already beginning to clear away the dinner dishes, her own nearly untouched plate included, sighed in defeat and sank back into her chair. Gloria Chatham might maintain control through her own basic good nature and femininity, but Rose Chatham had no time for the niceties. Age, she always said, had its privileges, a theory Elizabeth had been hearing from the woman as long as she could remember, and she knew she had only two choices open to her when Gammy gave an order.

She could sit down and answer the woman's

questions, or she could run away. The only problem was that she couldn't hide forever. Sooner or later her grandmother would find her and proceed to hurl embarrassing questions at her until she had ferreted out every last secret. With Gammy, nothing was sacred, and she had the tenacity of a bulldog when it came to getting her own way.

The fact that her oldest granddaughter had been living on her own for the past three years in Manhattan hadn't changed Rose's assumption that she was entitled to know about every facet of the young woman's life, and to have some say in whatever Elizabeth did. Elizabeth thought fleetingly of that saying "you can't go home again," and smiled. You could go home again, she decided, but only if you left your newfound independence on the doorstep.

She decided to give in early—at least this time—and save her energy for Gammy's reaction to what she had to say. "Yes, Gammy," Elizabeth agreed as the rest of her family escaped as quickly as they could. Holding her hands up in front of her as if trying to ward off blows, she whimpered, "Anything you say, copper. I'll talk, honest. Only please, no thumbscrews."

"Elizabeth, behave yourself," her mother warned quietly as she returned to the dining room to gather the last of the dinner dishes onto a tray. "Gammy's only being curious."

"Gammy's only being nosy, Mother," Elizabeth corrected, handing her mother a glass. "But I don't mind. She's old now, you know, and has to live vicariously through us."

"Elizabeth!" Gloria exclaimed, shocked, while Rose laughed out loud.

"Oh, Elizabeth," Rose complimented happily, "much as I love those three ruffians, you'll always be my favorite. You're just as sassy as I ever was. Gloria, close your mouth and go away. Your daughter and I have some catching up to do—don't we, dear? You went straight to work at Lancaster's the moment you moved back home, and I hardly ever see you. I knew more about you when you were kicking up your heels in New York. At least then I had your letters."

Elizabeth reached her hands across the lace tablecloth and squeezed her grandmother's heavily ringed fingers in her own. "I didn't mean to ignore you since I'm home, Gammy, but you know how it is in retailing. The hours are awful and, besides, I have a whole department to learn, a whole new system of doing things."

Gloria looked at her daughter and Rose without jealousy. She knew the two shared a special bond, and had since Rose had been widowed and moved in with her and Jack when Elizabeth was just about ten and Megan was a baby. Both of them had felt like displaced persons, Rose missing the husband she had lived with since she had been a girl of sixteen, and Elizabeth confused by the presence of a baby in the house. The two had been naturally drawn to each other.

When John and Paul had followed Megan into the world within three years, Gloria had been more than happy to have Rose's help with her oldest child. If she had missed out on some girlish confidences during Elizabeth's teenage years, Rose's renewed interest in life had made that loss easier to bear.

Gloria Chatham was a sensitive, loving woman, and her greatest happiness came in seeing those around her happy. Now, able to detect a slight glimmering of tears in Rose's eyes, she quietly withdrew into the kitchen, leaving the two good friends alone.

"So, child," Rose said after a few moments, "what's his name?"

Elizabeth withdrew her hands and laid them in her lap. Concentrating her gaze on her tightly clasped fingers she whispered, "Nicholas—Nicholas Lancaster."

"Nicholas Lancaster," Rose repeated quietly, her own hands sliding slowly from the tabletop and onto her lap. "Henry Lancaster's boy? How about that. Whoever would have thought it."

"You know Mr. Lancaster, Gammy? I understand he retired from Lancaster's a couple of years ago, although he still comes into the main store fairly often. Gee, I didn't think about it before, but the two of you must be about the same age. Did you go to school together? Is Mr. Lancaster one of the million boys who chased you until Grandpa caught you? Was he the one with the rumble seat? I'm all ears. Tell me *everything*!"

"Down, girl, down." Rose shook her head, banishing some private thought, and countered, "Don't think you can change the subject and start me off on one of my stories, young lady. So, this young man of yours is also your boss. You're my granddaughter through and through, starting right at the top. I've always said it's just as easy to love a rich man as it is to love a poor man, not that I would have traded your Grandpa for ten millionaires."

Elizabeth flushed hotly, her brown eyes flashing. "He's not my 'young man,' Gammy, and his being rich has nothing to do with it. Besides, we only had lunch together—a business lunch. Really, in a minute you'll be calling Father Chuck to have the banns posted."

"Is he handsome? As I recall, Henry Lancaster was quite a looker."

Elizabeth began tapping her heels agitatedly against the parquet floor beneath the table. "His face wouldn't exactly make little children run from him, screaming."

Rose grinned—wickedly, to Elizabeth's mind. "A regular Adonis, is he? And he's crazy about you, of course. Oh, to be young again!"

Suddenly it wasn't the same. Elizabeth had always confided in her grandmother, told her all about her dates, every detail of her conversations with her many boyfriends. But this was different. This was private; her feelings were too new, too intense to be shared, even with Rose. Jumping to her feet, Elizabeth declared airily, "You've been watching too many soap operas, Gammy. We met, we had lunch together in the store cafeteria, we're having dinner together tomorrow night. That's the beginning, the middle and the end of it. Honestly, Gammy, Nicholas Lancaster is just another date."

Rose stood up, carefully refolding her napkin and placing it back on the table. "We had roast beef, mashed potatoes and gravy for dinner tonight, Elizabeth," she intoned importantly, as if she were a prosecutor about to reveal an important piece of evidence. "Your all-time favorite. I made the gravy nice and dark, especially for you."

"My goodness," Elizabeth said warily, "now that's a news flash. So what?"

"Sooo," her grandmother replied, dragging out the word on purpose, "you only ate three teeny bites of meat and two forkfuls of potatoes. You didn't even touch the corn, but as you never were a good sport about your yellow vegetables, I won't count that against you. Besides, the meat and potatoes are evidence enough. You, my precious child, are in love."

"In love!" Elizabeth shouted, then quickly lowered her voice because, in the Chatham household, even the walls seemed to have ears. "In love?" she repeated much more softly. "Don't be ridiculous. So I didn't have much of an appetite tonight. Big deal. I don't think we'll have to alert the media. Maybe I just wasn't hungry. It happens, you know, impossible as that is for you to believe. Now please excuse me, I'm going to help Megan and Mother finish up in the kitchen."

"What's today's date, Elizabeth?" Rose asked as her granddaughter turned to escape from the room.

"September twelfth. Why?"

Rose walked around the table to reach up and kiss her granddaughter on the cheek. "Good. That gives us just about enough time. Christmas weddings are so romantic, don't you think?"

Elizabeth opened her mouth to speak, then closed it again, knowing there was no arguing with her grandmother once the woman got something into her head. Sometimes—almost all the time—it was easier, and less aggravating, to say nothing. Leaning down to return the woman's kiss, Elizabeth only whispered, "Bah, humbug, darling," before heading for the safety of the kitchen.

Rose watched her granddaughter's retreating back until the kitchen door swung closed behind her. "Hank Lancaster," she mused aloud. "Let's just hope the son's got as much gumption as the father."

Chapter Two

Nick was fairly certain the strip steak had been prepared just the way he liked it, but he couldn't have sworn to it, any more than he could remember if that had been orange or raspberry sherbet he and Elizabeth had shared for dessert.

As they walked across the nearly deserted parking lot to the car, Nick smiled in the darkness, the warm glow that had filled him from the moment he had met Elizabeth at the employee's entrance having multiplied a dozen times over as the evening progressed.

"The prime rib was really delicious, Mr. Lancaster," Elizabeth told him as they stopped on the passenger side of the car and he unlocked the door for her. ''I don't believe I've ever tasted better, even in New York. How was your steak?''

Nick opened the car door before answering, his forearm resting lightly against the roof as he faced her, effectively blocking her way. ''Beats me,'' he admitted honestly, frowning down at her. ''They could have put boiled shoe leather in front of me, for all the attention I was paying to what I ate. Elizabeth, we've been talking almost nonstop all evening, about anything and everything, right? So, tell me; why don't you call me by my first name?''

''Why don't I...well, um, I...after all, you're my...that is to say, we've really only just met, and—'' She stopped talking and hung her head before adding, ''Feel free to stop me at any time, okay?''

Nick lifted her chin with one finger, freeing her face from the sleek curtain of hair that had fallen forward to hide her perfect features. ''The workday ended for us at six o'clock. Your boss didn't ask you out to dinner, Elizabeth, I did. Allow me to introduce myself. The name is Lancaster. Nicholas Charles Lancaster, actually, but my friends call me Nick. Hello, Elizabeth.''

Tilting her head to one side, Elizabeth smiled up at him, her brown eyes twinkling with amusement. Her voice suddenly lower, huskier, breathier, she said, ''Well, hello there yourself—Nick.''

He had always been rather indifferent to his name, thinking it ordinary and not all that spectacular, but when he heard his name on Elizabeth's lips, suddenly it sounded important, even majestic. Swallowing hard, Nick pushed himself away from the car and slid his arms lightly around Elizabeth's back. "Promise me you won't scream, please. I've been longing to do this from the first moment we met."

"I—I prom—" Elizabeth said on a sigh, her eyelids fluttering closed as his mouth descended slowly, searching for hers, only to pop open wide as his warm lips claimed hers, setting off an instantaneous explosion deep inside her body. She was overwhelmed with sensation, and a sudden physical weakness enveloped her, causing her eyelids to close once more and her knees to wobble. Raising her trembling hands to his shoulders, she clung to him as her world narrowed to exclude all but the two of them.

She fit into his arms perfectly, her lips molded to precisely the right shape beneath his, her softness complementing his lean, muscular frame. She was his other half. She made him whole. She was the reason he had been born; his reason to go on living. He loved her—had loved this woman from the moment he first saw her.

And if he told her all this now she'd probably

call a cop and have him locked up. Nick withdrew his lips a fraction, his embrace slackening as he prepared to back away and put some sanity-inducing space between them. He was being Noble Nick, he told himself, he was being civilized.

But then he made one small mistake. With their faces only inches apart, he opened his eyes and looked straight into hers. She was looking at him with her heart laid bare, with all her secrets revealed and his for the taking. He realized that she had felt it, too, this wild, unbelievably sweet communion.

"Again, Elizabeth," he whispered hoarsely, not even aware he had spoken, and once more they kissed each other, held each other, alone together in the dark, the rest of the world forgotten.

"You have the latest sales figures for the Baltimore branch yet, Nick?" Henry Lancaster sat at one end of the long conference table, his back to his son. When there was no answer to his question he swiveled in his seat to see Nick standing in front of the floor-to-ceiling window, staring out over the city. "Nicholas, wake up. You're woolgathering again. It has to be a woman. What's her name?"

His father's words rudely interrupting his pleasant daydream, Nick reluctantly moved away from the window and walked back over to the conference table, resting his palms against the gleaming teak surface as he leaned forward and looked into his father's astonishingly bright blue eyes. "Tell me something, Dad. How did you know that you were in love with Mother? I mean, *really* in love?"

"*Really* in love? Well now, let me think about that for a minute." Henry sat back in the plush leather chair, cupping his hands behind his neck as a slow, warm smile softened his thin, angular features. He thought for a few moments, his smile growing wider, then said, "It was fairly easy, actually, Nick. Your mother told me."

Shaking his head, Nick laughed out loud. "Mother? Shy, quiet Mother? I can't picture it."

Henry rose and walked over to the window. He stood staring through the glass as his son had done a few minutes earlier, his eyes narrowed as if he were watching a movie unroll in front of him, a private screening of his most cherished memories. "Your mother was quite a woman, Nick, quite a lady. Genteel, well-bred and polite to a fault. But that didn't mean she was weak. Oh no, on the contrary. She was no shrinking violet, and she wasn't afraid to fight to get what she wanted."

"Fight, Dad? Are you sure you're talking about *my* mother?" Nick teased lovingly, as his memories of his mother always centered around visions of the woman sitting at the grand piano in the living room, or arranging homegrown flowers in a cut crystal vase, or presiding at an elegant dinner party. "What did she do, flip you for who got to pop the question?"

Henry turned his head in his son's direction and Nick could clearly see the love the older man still held for the wife who had died ten years earlier. "Your mother and I dated for nearly two years, although I only saw her once a week, on Saturday nights. Your grandfather's business was just getting off the ground, and I was working almost around the clock. Anyway, I think she had begun to believe I was taking her for granted, you know, believing she'd always be there, waiting for me to have the time to see her, and she decided to do something about it."

Nick rubbed a hand across his chin, remembering that, no matter the season, no matter how busy the business was, his father was always home by six o'clock to have dinner with his wife and son and spend his evenings with them. "I take it she found a way to change your lifestyle."

"That she did, son," Henry replied with a chuckle. "For three straight weeks your mother was 'unavailable,' until I couldn't work, I couldn't eat, I couldn't sleep—all I could do was think of her. When she finally agreed to see me she sat me down and explained that I loved her, and it was time we started talking about getting married. It's a good thing she didn't wait any longer to pop the question, too, even if the war did keep us apart for four years. As it was, it took us more than fifteen years to produce you.''

Nick gave a low whistle of appreciation. ''So Mother actually proposed to you? I can't believe it.''

''Believe it, Nick,'' Henry declared, going over to put his arm around his son's shoulders. ''Your mother and Rosie O'Hanlon—between the two of them, I didn't stand a chance.''

''Who's Rosie O'Hanlon?''

Henry smiled again, conjuring up a mental picture of his wife's next-door neighbor all those years ago. ''Lord, I haven't thought about Rosie in years. Now there was a young lady who knew what she wanted and went after it until she got it. Married at sixteen or some such nonsense, I believe your mother heard later. It wasn't unusual then for girls to leave school and start families at that age. I'll bet the poor fellow never knew what hit him. Anyway, Rosie aided and abetted your mother in the whole scheme, although your mother didn't let me in on that little secret until our tenth anniversary, of course. But, let me tell you, I never regretted being tricked—not for a single moment of all our years together.''

Nick's hazel eyes clouded as he thought about his mother. "She was a great lady, Dad. I believe I miss her almost as much as you do."

Henry sighed, gave his son's back a few gentle pats and resumed his seat. "So, now that we've had that little trip down memory lane, tell me—what's her name?"

Nick's smile was glowing. "Elizabeth."

Henry nodded consideringly. "Elizabeth, huh. Nice. She have a last name?"

"What?" At the mention of her name, Nick had slipped once more into a pleasant daydream. "Oh, of course. Sorry, Dad. Her name is Chatham. Elizabeth Chatham. She's our new housewares buyer."

"Chatham…Chatham," Henry repeated, mulling the name over in his mind. "Sounds familiar, but I can't place it right now. So, you want me to tell you if you're in love, is that it? You're nearly thirty-two years old, Nick. I doubt if this could be puppy love. How long have you known this Elizabeth?"

"Two weeks today," Nick admitted, knowing two weeks wasn't a very long time—especially to a man who had dated for over two years and still had to be shocked into proposing. "But we've seen each other nearly every night. I'd like you to meet her, Dad. She's really wonderful."

Henry looked at his only son, who appeared as

earnest as he had as a young boy trying to talk him into buying a puppy, and felt an unfamiliar tightening in his chest. Nick had dated dozens of young women over the years, but he'd never brought any of them home. This Elizabeth Chatham must be some young woman.

"I think Friday evening would be fine, Nick. I'll have Mrs. Gillespie fix something really special. Now why don't you go downstairs and check with Ms. Chatham to see if it's all right with her, while I try to find those Baltimore sales figures. One of us has to keep his mind on the job, you know, and from the look on your face I can see I won't get a lick of work out of you until you've talked to her."

Nick's face split into a wide grin as he pushed a thick manila file toward his father and quickly headed for the door. "Thanks, Dad. I'll be back in fifteen minutes, twenty minutes, tops—I promise."

Pulling the folder in front of him, Henry folded his hands on top of it and opened his heart to memories of his wife, his smile wistful, yet happy. "She may be wonderful, this Elizabeth," he whispered aloud in the quiet room, "but she'll have to go some to hold a candle to you, my darling Katherine."

Elizabeth was lying on her back underneath the frilly white eyelet canopy that, since her earliest memories, had transformed her ordinary bed into a fairy-tale land whenever she wished. A gift from her grandmother, the high, wide four-poster bed had served as a comforting refuge when the world got to be too much for her—her quiet "thinking place." And when she drew the floor-length draperies around the bed, nobody was allowed to disturb her, except for her grandmother, of course, who had always been welcome.

But not tonight. Tonight Elizabeth wanted, needed, to be alone. She had disappeared upstairs as quickly as possible after helping with the dinner dishes, feeling Gammy's too-observant eyes on her all through the meal, so that she had choked down every bit of food on her plate, even the green beans, which she had always hated.

The last thing she needed was for Gammy to give her another third-degree grilling about her poor appetite and Nicholas Lancaster. After two weeks of Elizabeth's seeing him every day at work and nearly every night for dinner, Gammy was already walking around the house humming the "Wedding March." It was embarrassing.

Not only was the situation embarrassing, but it was confusing. Elizabeth's entire life had been disrupted, and she had let it happen. She knew that she had allowed herself to be totally absorbed in Nick, to the exclusion of anything and anybody else. John had complained only that morning that Elizabeth had missed his first freshman basketball game after promising to attend, and Megan had scolded her for failing to take her shopping at Lancaster's for a new pair of jeans.

Elizabeth squirmed uncomfortably on the mattress, feeling guilty. Some sister she was. She had moved back home because she'd missed her family, and yet now she was farther away from them than when she had worked in New York City and traveled home by bus one weekend every month.

Her parents hadn't said anything to her so far, but Elizabeth had seen the concern in her mother's eyes. *They think I'm moving too fast,* Elizabeth decided silently, *and they just might be right. I don't know what's going on, how I feel, even how I should feel. This is all so new, so different, for me to understand it.*

"Hi, Liz." Megan's voice was a plaintive whine. "I can come in, can't I? I mean, you don't have the curtains pulled or anything."

Elizabeth's first reaction was to remind her sister that, even if the bed's draperies were open, the door to her room had been closed, but she stopped herself in time and only said, "Sure, Meg, come on in. I was only resting my legs for a few minutes. The worst thing about retailing is being on your feet all day. There was a one-day sale today and I had to help out on the floor.''

"Oh. Gee, that's rough. I'm sorry." Megan stared at the tip of her left sneaker, the one she was digging into the deep rose shag rug.

Elizabeth looked blank for a moment, then sat up and slapped a hand against her forehead as the realization hit her. ''Your jeans! Lancaster's is open late tonight because of the sale and you want me to take you over there—oh, Meggie, of course I will. I'm just sorry I didn't think of it myself.''

Megan brightened instantly, her freckled face rosy with pleasure. ''And that dopey Paulie said you wouldn't take me! Oh, Liz, you're the best sister ever! I'll hunt up Dad's keys and meet you at the car. You'll just love the jeans I want. They're just like my friend Sandy's—all faded and with holes in the knees—really neat!''

Collapsing back down on her pillows, Elizabeth gave a weak laugh. Megan already owned a half-dozen pairs of faded jeans with holes in them. The only thing wrong with them was that those weren't designer holes, they were only old-age holes. As much as Elizabeth hated to admit it, sometimes it seemed true—people would buy anything, as long as it was considered fashionable.

''No wonder I like the housewares department,'' she mused, searching under the bed for her sneakers. "There's no such thing as a designer potato peeler. Of course," she added consideringly, "there *are* all those fancy food processors that do everything but sit up and—"

"Liz!" Megan's screech swooped up the stairwell and into the bedroom. "I've got Dad's car keys. You coming or what?"

Two hours later, their booth loaded with bright blue-and-white striped plastic shopping bags, Megan and Elizabeth sat in the store restaurant, Elizabeth sipping a cup of coffee while watching her sister devour a double-dutch hot-fudge sundae.

"You sure you don't want a bite, Liz?" Megan asked, licking a dollop of fudge from the back of the spoon. "This is really great."

"Hmm?" Elizabeth had been quietly observing a small group of men sitting at a table in the far corner of the restaurant. His back was turned to her, but she was sure Nick was one of them. He had told her he had an important business meeting tonight. "Uh, no thanks, Meg," she said as her sister repeated her offer, stiffening slightly when the four men rose politely as a beautifully dressed redhead joined them at the table. "I'm not hungry."

Megan peered inquiringly at her sister, then turned around in her chair to see what had put such a sad look on Elizabeth's face. "Wow! Why can't

I do that with my hair, Liz? Do you think this stupid red frizz will ever look all warm and coppery like that? Do you think she's a model or something?''

The redhead slid off the forest-green wool coat she had worn into the restaurant and the man Elizabeth had thought was Nick signaled for a waitress to take it. It *was* Nick, and the redhead was sitting down right beside him, her beautiful, perfectly made-up face raised beguilingly as she thanked him for holding her chair.

''Red and green,'' Elizabeth muttered nastily. ''How perfectly ordinary. The woman has no imagination, no imagination at all.''

''Gee, Liz,'' Megan leaned across the table to whisper eagerly, ''you sound real angry. Do you know that woman or something?''

Realizing that she was being petty, Elizabeth firmly returned her gaze to the table and her sister. ''No, I don't know her, Megan. I was just being catty—and stupid. Please forgive me.''

Megan took another spoonful of her sundae. ''Oh, darn, Liz, don't go getting all stuffy on me. Come on, you can tell me. Is she one of your Nick Lancaster's old girlfriends? Tell me all the dirt.''

Elizabeth propped her elbow on the table and her chin in her hand. Looking once more toward the table in the corner, she grumbled, ''I don't know, and I don't care. And he's not *my* Nicholas Lancaster.''

Now Megan laughed out loud. ''Oh, brother, Gammy was right—you have got it *bad*! When are you going to bring this guy home so we can meet him? You always go out straight from here. Mom's beginning to think you're ashamed of us, but Gammy said if Dad promises to chain John and Paul in the basement she's sure you'll bring him home someday. Liz, you look strange. What's wrong?''

Elizabeth sat up straight and spread her napkin more fully over her lap, trying to hide her old jeans. ''You want to meet Nick Lancaster, Megan? Well, don't look now, but he's coming this way. Do I look all right?''

''He's coming this—where? Which one of them is he? Do you look all right? Of course you do. You always do. How do I look? Is he really coming over here? What color is his hair? Is he wearing a—''

''Hello, Elizabeth.'' Nick's voice was low, intimate, and to Megan's ears obviously extremely sexy. ''I thought I saw you sitting over here.''

''—suit?'' Megan finished on a sigh, looking up at Nick, her mouth opened wide. *''Oh, wow,''* she gushed, too quietly for Nick to hear her over the low hum of conversation in the crowded restaurant.

"Hello, Nicholas," Elizabeth answered, wishing her voice didn't sound so thin, so strained. What was the matter with her? She was reacting even more immaturely than her teenage sister. "I thought I saw you earlier, when we first came in. Is your meeting over?"

Waving his companions on their way and promising to catch up with them in a few minutes, Nick pulled out a chair and sat down beside Elizabeth before introducing himself to Megan. "Elizabeth has told me all about you, Megan," he offered, smiling down at the girl who was staring at him as if he had suddenly grown an extra head. "You're on the school newspaper, aren't you?"

Megan swallowed with obvious difficulty. "Feature—er, I'm the feature editor."

"Oh, really?" Nicholas responded, looking toward Elizabeth. "You know, several years ago Lancaster's worked with many of the local high-school papers, using our Junior World fashions for models chosen by the feature editor for newspaper articles three or four times a year. We supplied our store photographer for the pictures and each feature editor wrote up the copy. We did sport clothes— for both boys and girls—and trendy wear and, in the spring, prom gowns. It was really very successful. Megan, do you think your adviser would like to try the idea again?"

Elizabeth was worried that she might have to reach across the table and physically restrain her sister from grabbing Nick and covering him with kisses.

"Would it?" Megan shrieked, her cornflower-blue eyes wide with excitement. "Oh, wow! Mr. German will really freak! I mean, he'll just jump at the—I mean, I'm sure Mr. German will consider it, Mr. Lancaster. And *I'd* get to pick the models and write the stories? Oh, Liz, I could pick Sandy, and Marcie, and—"

"I know I'm going out on a limb here, Nick, but I think she likes the idea," Elizabeth interrupted dryly before adding, "You don't have to do this, you know."

"The series was very effective, as I recall, Elizabeth, and Megan's school probably won't be the only one I contact," he assured her before rising once more and reaching into his jacket pocket for his business card. "Megan, you have Mr. German phone me and we'll arrange the first session, all right?"

Nick then shook her hand, once more reducing Megan to unintelligible monosyllables, and she could barely choke out a polite thank-you before holding the business card in front of her with both hands and staring at it as if it were printed on purest gold.

"Elizabeth," he went on, looking down at her, "I really have to go now. I have to show Mrs. Halstead around the jewelry department."

Elizabeth ran her tongue around her dry lips. He was talking about the beautiful redhead. "Mrs. Halstead? Is she interested in jewelry?"

Nick smiled and the last of the ice melted from around Elizabeth's heart. "I guess you could say that, sweetheart. She and her husband own one of the largest freshwater pearl outlets in the country. He's home nursing a sprained back and she's been sent to scout us out, to see if Lancaster's is worthy of their product. I think she's pretty impressed so far, but I don't want to leave her alone with the vice presidents too long."

"No, no, of course not!" Elizabeth suddenly felt wonderful, as if she had just taken in a refreshing lungful of sweet spring air. "You'd better not keep her waiting."

"I'll see you for lunch tomorrow as usual?"

Elizabeth's smile faded. They had lunched together almost every day, either by accident or design, but tomorrow was her day off and she had promised she would help her grandmother can the last of this season's tomatoes before going to John's basketball game right after school. "I can't," she said at last, her disappointment obvious.

"Oh," Nick commented hollowly, causing Megan to look at her sister and wink. "Well then, I'll just have to wait until tomorrow night. Dad said to come around seven, if that's all right with you?"

"I'll be ready," she assured him, then watched him as he made his way through the tables and out of the restaurant.

"You'll be ready, all right," Megan said. "God, Liz, why didn't you tell me he was such a hunk?"

Elizabeth's smile was dreamy as she turned back to face her sister. "Yes, he is, isn't he?"

"Oh, Lordy!" Megan derided before downing the last of her cola. "Gammy sure called it right this time. You're crazy about the guy, Liz. And you know what? I think he's crazy about you, too."

"Don't read too much into this, Meg," Elizabeth warned, aware that her heart had skipped a beat at her sister's words. "We've only been seeing each other for a couple of weeks."

"Sure," Megan shot back. "And you wanted to pull that redhead's hair out because you don't like green coats. Cut me a break here, Liz. My sister's gone bonkers for Nicholas Lancaster. Gee, do you think if you marry him he'll let our whole family use the employee discount?"

"Megan, my dearest sister," Elizabeth said woodenly, "shut up and eat your ice cream."

Chapter Three

"Nervous?"

Elizabeth fought her way into the buttercup-yellow silk-and-angora-blend sweater, her head finally poking through the proper opening so that her chestnut curls bounced free to swirl around her face. "Nervous, Gammy?" she repeated on a slight laugh, carefully adjusting the sweater's three-quarter-length sleeves. "Nervous doesn't even begin to cover it. I'm terrified! There, that does it. I bought this outfit last night when I went shopping with Megan. What do you think?"

Rose Chatham sat on the edge of the high mattress, her slim legs lazily swinging back and forth a good ten inches above the floor. "You look like a pretty statue carved out of freshly churned butter, Elizabeth; good enough to eat. That muted shade of yellow has always been a good color for you. But,'' she offered kindly, ''I do think it would look even better if you wore the skirt. Warmer, too.''

Elizabeth pulled a face at her grandmother's teasing, snatched the sweater-knit skirt from the bed, and stepped into it. After donning the long matching cardigan and slipping her ivory-stockinged feet into slim bone-colored heels she stepped back to give Rose the full effect of the ensemble.

''All right, now what do you think? This outfit cost me a full week's salary, Gammy, even with my employee discount, so please, be gentle.''

Rose hopped down from the bed and walked around her granddaughter, inspecting her from every angle. Elizabeth was a stunningly beautiful young woman, both inside and out, but tonight she positively glowed. *If Hank Lancaster does anything to burst this child's bubble,* Rose decided, *I will personally cut his heart out!*

''Well? Do I pass muster, Gammy?'' Elizabeth asked when her grandmother didn't speak.

''You look wonderful, Elizabeth—*almost* as pretty as I did the day I caught your grandfather,'' Rose assured her, ''except for one small thing.''

Elizabeth raced over to the free-standing brass

mirror and peered into it intently. "What is it? Do I look pale? I still have to put on my lipstick, but I was afraid I'd get some on the sweater."

"A little war paint wouldn't hurt," Rose agreed, "but that wasn't what I meant. You go sit at your vanity table and fix your lips, Elizabeth, and I'll be right back."

Elizabeth watched as her grandmother left the room, then did as she was told, carefully blotting her lips on a tissue just as Rose came up behind her and told her to close her eyes.

Stiffening slightly as she felt Rose's hands lift her hair to fasten something behind her neck, Elizabeth opened her eyes to see her grandmother's treasured single-strand pearl necklace lying against the soft knit of her sweater. "Oh, Gammy," she breathed, overcome with emotion, "these are the pearls Grandpa gave you on your last wedding anniversary before he—I can't wear this! What if the string broke? What if I lost all the pearls?"

"You won't lose them," Rose insisted, handing Elizabeth the matching drop earrings and watching while she put them on. "Besides, if you did, I'd just forgive you like the wonderful woman I am, and then I'd throw this lovely new outfit in the clothes dryer—on High. No, I'm just kidding. Really, dear, I'm not worried a bit."

Elizabeth put up a hand to settle the necklace

more smoothly around her throat and then touched her fingers to her ears. "They're the most beautiful pearls I've ever seen, such a rich, creamy shade. Grandpa always had excellent taste—in women as well as jewelry."

Rose dropped a kiss on the top of Elizabeth's head and then quickly turned away, memories of her late husband making her eyes slightly misty. "I always intended them for you on your wedding day anyway, but I don't want you going to Henry Lancaster's looking anything but your best. Now stop that sniffling before we both make fools of ourselves. Besides, I thought I just heard a car door, and I want to give this Nick of yours the once-over. Just because your parents are out at that bowling banquet doesn't mean this Lancaster fellow is going to think there's no one here who gives two hoots about how late he brings you home."

Elizabeth blew her nose and gave a small laugh. "Do you remember my first really 'grown-up' date, Gammy?" she asked, giving Rose a quick hug, which she knew was all her grandmother would tolerate.

"Tommy Something-or-other, if my memory serves," Rose recalled, checking her own appearance in the full-length mirror and deciding that, for an old lady, she didn't look that bad. "A basketball player, like your brother John, wasn't he? All skinny legs and hip pockets, and a shirt collar three sizes too big for him.''

"Please, Gammy," Elizabeth protested, laughing. "I'll have you know that Tommy Rothenberger was only the biggest catch in the entire junior class. All my girlfriends were green with envy.''

"Which doesn't say much for your junior class," Rose sniffed, giving her short curly hair a last pat. "But I do remember the third degree your father gave that poor boy. I wonder if he ever fully recovered."

"'Do you own a car, son?' he asked," Elizabeth recited, mimicking Jack Chatham's deep, gruff voice. "And when poor Tommy admitted that his car was parked out front, Dad really went on the attack. 'So, you drive, do you? Do you drive *fast*?' Honestly, by the time Dad was done, all I wanted to do was find a great big hole and hide in it. Tommy had me home by ten and never called again. I thought my life was over. I hated Dad for weeks."

The doorbell rang and Elizabeth and Rose exchanged quick looks, their calming reminiscences immediately forgotten as Elizabeth nervously bit her lip and her grandmother reminded her granddaughter that she had supposedly outgrown that particular bad habit at the age of twelve.

"Hey, Lizzie," Paul's squeaky, half-grown-up

voice bellowed from the narrow foyer, "your date's here. You comin' down or what?"

"So refined, so delicate. So absolutely elegant," Rose commented, her smile wry. "Remind me to have a talk with that boy, Elizabeth; perhaps my were-you-raised-in-a-barn? speech. Now let's go downstairs quickly, before Paul and John decide to try a duet."

Taking up her new bone-colored leather envelope purse and a stylish mohair wool cape she had picked up that past year at Bloomingdale's for a song, Elizabeth walked toward the stairs, Rose close on her heels, only to stop, one hand on the dark mahogany bannister. "You are going to behave, Gammy, aren't you? I mean, I really like Nick, but he's an only child, and I don't think he's used to a madhouse like ours."

Rose looked at her granddaughter, looking so self-assured, so sophisticated—so New York—and saw through to the frightened little girl hiding beneath that sophistication. "And you're politely telling me you don't want me to scare him off. Don't worry, I know how important this young man is to you, honey. After all, he's the first person to ever come between us, isn't he?"

Elizabeth's eyes clouded at the unexpected sadness that had crept into her grandmother's voice. "Oh, Gammy, Nick hasn't come between us! Nobody could! I know I haven't come creeping into your room at midnight to tell you all about our dates like I used to, but that's because there's something different about it this time. I can't explain it, but I guess I'm being selfish with my happiness—and maybe even a little superstitious. I don't think I'm ready to share Nick yet, not even with you. I don't feel right talking about our time together; I don't know why. Please, Gammy, try to understand.''

''I do understand, my darling,'' Rose answered softly. ''I really do, and that's probably why I'm a little sad, even though I'm also very happy for you. Now, go on downstairs and rescue poor Nick before Megan tries to work her wiles on him. She hasn't been able to stop talking about your Nick since she came home last night. If you don't watch it, you'll have all the Chatham women falling in love with him. In fact, just to be safe, I think I'll stay up here.''

Elizabeth kissed her grandmother again, frowning. ''Then you aren't coming downstairs after all? I don't understand. You said you were anxious to meet Nick. Gammy, are you sure you aren't angry with me?''

Rose dismissed Elizabeth's question with a wave of her hand. ''No, dear, I'm not angry. I've just decided that Nick Lancaster might be better off if he took his Chathams in small doses at first. I'm sure I'll soon get to see him a dozen times a week, if this dinner party at his father's means what I think it does.''

Elizabeth was sidetracked, as her grandmother wanted her to be. ''Oh, Gammy, there you go again, dreaming silly dreams. Anyone would think you've already picked out names for your first great-grandchild.''

''John Henry after your grandfather and Nick's father if it's a boy—even if it does make him sound like a railroad engineer—and Katherine Anne, after Nick's mother and your maternal grandmother if it's a girl,'' Rose quipped immediately, winking at Elizabeth before turning around and heading back down the hall to her small combination bedroom and private sitting room.

''How did you know Nick's mother's name?'' Elizabeth called after her, careful to keep her voice low. ''Just how well do you know Henry Lancaster?''

Rose stopped, turned around and wagged a finger at her granddaughter. ''As I told you when you were eleven and you wanted to know how babies are made—*I* know everything, but that doesn't mean I have to tell *you* any more than you need to know. Have a wonderful time tonight, Elizabeth. You never looked more beautiful.''

Putting out one foot to start her descent to the foyer and Nick, Elizabeth warned, "Just don't you dare fall asleep before I get home, Gammy. I want to tell you all about my evening. I *really* do."

Rose closed the door to her small apartment behind her, leaned against it, raised her eyes to the ceiling and spoke to her late husband. "Elizabeth and that young man are getting married, whether they know it yet or not. I can see the same look in that girl's eyes that I saw in yours when you came courting all those years ago. And I'll tell you something else, John; that girl is going to have the wedding you and I missed—the biggest, grandest wedding this town has ever seen. I can promise you that because I'm going to see to it, *personally*!"

It was quiet in the car as Nick turned onto Prospect Avenue and headed north on the narrow, tree-lined street. When they reached the intersection at Eighth Avenue, Elizabeth absently turned her head to look at the rambling, three-story brick-and-stucco Tudor house that had fascinated her since childhood.

"Oh, Nick, I just can't believe it," she was startled into saying. "When could that have happened? They're selling my house!"

Nick slowed the car to make the turn onto

Eighth Avenue, then looked to his left to see the realtor's sign in the front yard of the house that sat on the southwest corner. "Your house, Elizabeth? That's funny; I thought we just left your house a minute ago. Or did you just hire those people to pretend to be your family?" he questioned lightly, before seeing her wistful expression.

"That was my family, all right," Elizabeth answered, twisting in her seat to look back at the house, "or at least as many of them that were home. Mom and Dad went to his bowling banquet and my grandmother stayed upstairs, er, resting." She turned forward in her seat once more with a sigh. "That house back there is my dream castle."

They didn't speak again for a while, as Nick could see that Elizabeth was lost in thought, her smooth brow furrowed. He left her alone, happy that she felt comfortable enough with him after the past two weeks to allow an occasional lapse in conversation. "Your dream castle? Sounds interesting," Nick said at last, interrupting her thoughts as they turned onto Macada Drive to enter an area Elizabeth knew to be very exclusive.

"Yes, it is, actually," Elizabeth agreed, willing to talk about the house if it would keep her from worrying about her upcoming meeting with Henry Lancaster, for with the turn into the residential area all her fears for the evening had returned. "Years ago, when the executives of Bethlehem Steel and other companies built their mansions, Prospect Avenue was what this area is now, not that it isn't still grand. But of all the beautiful houses, the Tudor always seemed to draw my attention.''

Nick glanced over at Elizabeth and nearly ran the car into a ditch, as his attention was immediately grabbed by the expression on her face, the way her wide brown eyes had gone dark and soft with emotion. *Does she look like that when she thinks of me?* he asked himself silently, praying that she did. "Like a giant-size dollhouse?''

Elizabeth laughed, the sound pleasant to Nick's ears. "Probably. When I was little it absolutely fascinated me, what with its three-story stone turret and all those oddly placed mullion windows. There just has to be a second-floor gallery, if those windows in the middle of the house mean anything.

"Anyway,'' she continued, "Gammy and I would walk past it all the time when we were out for what she still calls her 'constitutional,' and she'd make up stories about the people who lived there. It's silly, but I almost think the owners should have asked my permission before putting it on the market.''

Nick pulled the car into a long, curving driveway and cut the engine in front of his father's house before sliding an arm across the back of

Elizabeth's bucket seat. "Do you want to satisfy your fantasy, Elizabeth?"

She turned to him, confused. "How? I doubt they'll open a house like that to the public."

Suddenly Nick felt all-powerful, like a magical genie who wanted nothing more than to grant this beautiful princess her every wish. "No, I don't think the realtor will need to do anything like that, but I can call and get us an appointment for a private showing."

Elizabeth didn't know what to say, how to react. It was one thing to joke about such an idea, but if the two of them were really going to look at houses—well, that sounded serious. Gammy would be delirious, for one thing, and she herself would have a hard time believing that Nick could still be classified as "just a date."

Besides, if she accepted, would she be sending him the wrong message? Would she be tacitly admitting that she loved him and wanted to marry him—or even worse, that she had decided the time was right to get married and he looked like acceptable husband material? Why hadn't they answered this sort of question in any of the how-to articles women's magazines were so fond of printing?

"Well, what do you say?" Nick prompted as Elizabeth remained silent, worried that he was moving too fast and wondering if she were trying to find a polite way of telling him to go peddle his papers somewhere else.

Elizabeth blinked twice, trying to bring Nick's face back into focus. He was so dear, sitting there with such an earnest, appealing expression; so unlike the corporate image he projected at Lancaster's. Her assistant, Judy Holland, wouldn't recognize him. Nicholas Lancaster was a *nice man*, and he was offering to do a nice thing. She was simply reading too much into a very mundane exercise. The house was for sale. They would look at the house. It was simple, very black-and-white. No strings attached.

"It certainly would be different," she said at last, her decision made. "Why not—let's do it!" Her heart skipped a beat as Nick showed his agreement by way of a long, slow, satisfying kiss.

Dinner had been wonderfully uneventful, with Henry Lancaster at home in the role of host, although he would never quite get used to seeing the empty chair facing him at the opposite end of the long dining-room table.

Henry had been openly pleased with Elizabeth, whom he had decided was not only beautiful but extremely intelligent, and their discussion of Lord Byron's *Don Juan* had lasted straight through the dessert course, with Nick surprised to find himself feeling the slightest twinge of jealousy as he had watched Elizabeth walk back into the living room on his father's arm.

Three hours later, after suffering through his father's proud exhibition of his son's baby pictures, Nick and Elizabeth were alone once more, walking hand in hand through the extensive rose garden Nick's mother had planted when he was a child.

"This reminds me of some of the English gardens I saw when I was in London last year on a buying trip. Even now, this late in the season, it's absolutely breathtaking." Elizabeth stopped beside a small statue of a cherub holding a water pitcher on his shoulder. "Oh, what a shame. Look, Nick, its nose is missing."

Nick slipped his arm around her back and Elizabeth instinctively snuggled against him. "I was afraid you might notice that. It's a remnant of my terrible youth, I'm ashamed to say."

"Aw, you did it with your little baseball," Elizabeth teased, looking up into his face in the faint light coming from the patio.

"Nope," Nick responded, flicking the tip of her nose with his finger. "I cannot tell a lie; I did it with my little slingshot. I was deadly within fifty feet."

Elizabeth pulled herself away just enough to turn

and face him, her hands now resting on his elbows as his arms lightly encircled her waist. "Your slingshot? You're kidding! Oh, please, don't ever tell John or Paul; I can't bear to think of the consequences."

Nick promised to keep the slingshot incident secret and they walked on, farther from the patio and deeper into the darkness. Elizabeth, her head resting lightly against his shoulder, took a deep breath of the crisp night air and her pulse leaped as a hint of his spicy cologne teased her nostrils. Involuntarily, she shivered.

"Cold?" Nick tightened his arm around her shoulders, his fingers taking delight in the softness of her sweater as he ran his hand rhythmically up and down her arm, a movement that sent another chill racing through her body. "We should go back to the house."

Trying to hide her disappointment, Elizabeth agreed, saying, "And then I probably should go home. I have to work tomorrow, you know, and my boss is a real stickler for having his employees arrive at work on time."

Nick's voice was low and menacing as he said, "Sounds like a real jerk, lady. Do ya want me ta take care of him for ya?"

Elizabeth laughed, shaking her head. This wasn't the first time they had playacted; both of them seemed to be able to speak their minds more freely if they made a game of it. Playing the game made Elizabeth happy, even while the need for it made her sad. "Oh, no, thank you, mister gangster, sir. You see, I may seem silly to you, but, I sorta like the guy."

"Oh, yeah, lady?" Nick pursued, staying in character. "Well, from what I hear from the boys in the mob, he sorta likes you, too. And that's no line," he ended in his own voice, although it sounded deeper and somewhat husky, even to his own ears.

They had kissed often since their first embrace in the parking lot of the restaurant, but by unspoken agreement they had been careful to limit those kisses to just before saying good-night. Their attraction had been too immediate, too electric, and it had been as if they were both holding back, determined to get to know each other better before allowing this powerful physical attraction to take control and overcome their better judgment.

They weren't teenagers who were falling in love with love. Elizabeth may have worried about that for a while, because she knew she had reached an age where her body was telling her it was time to find a mate, but this was only a vague self-imposed caution. In her heart she knew that this time it was different. This time it was right.

Nick had also been restraining his urge to claim Elizabeth for his own. He had been involved with other women over the years, had even thought he was in love a few times. But meeting Elizabeth had done something to him, had awakened feelings inside him that were foreign to him, and even a little bit frightening. It was as if he wanted to build a high fence around Elizabeth and post a warning against trespassers. He felt an almost overriding need to lay claim to her, to shout to the world that this woman—this wonderful, marvelous, perfect woman—was his, and his alone.

He hadn't needed his father's approval; Nick had been his own man for more than a dozen years. He hadn't taken Elizabeth home to meet his father as if she were some prize he had won or a beautiful art object he wished to have admired. If his father had hated Elizabeth on sight it would have hurt Nick, but it wouldn't have changed his high opinion of her.

He liked Elizabeth. He admired her. He felt comfortable with her. He felt alive with her. He wanted her. "Oh, hell," he said out loud as they stood so close together in his mother's night-dark garden, "I love her!"

Elizabeth, her mind working along much the same lines as his, gasped almost inaudibly and asked, "What—what did you say?"

Nick shut his eyes a moment, realizing he had spoken his last thought aloud. "I think I just said that I love you," he told her, feeling himself drowning in her large, trusting eyes and cheerfully going down for the third time.

Elizabeth bit her bottom lip, then nodded. "That—that's what I thought you said." *So now what, Elizabeth?* she screamed silently. *This is all happening so fast—maybe too fast. What do you do now?*

Nick saw the sudden confusion in Elizabeth's eyes. "I'm way ahead of you, aren't I, darling? I'm sorry."

"No...no! That's not it," Elizabeth protested, then fell silent. *Tell him, you idiot!* Her inner voice was screaming at her, while her tongue refused to move. It was like one of her childhood nightmares, the one where she was in danger but couldn't cry out. *You love him; you know you love him. Say something, for goshsakes! If you go home and tell Gammy what a dope you're being she'll have you locked up!*

"Yes, it is," Nick persisted, "and I don't blame you. To tell you the truth, I rather surprised myself. Why don't we just drop it for now, okay?"

Elizabeth nodded vigorously, wondering if she had lost her voice forever, only to find it in time to say something so honest, so revealing, that it immediately made her cheeks hot with embarrassed color. "It's a deal, Nick. Now, how about we kiss on it, just to make it official?"

"Anything you say, Elizabeth," Nick agreed, relief in his voice. "Your wish is my command."

The teasing was back—the harmless game playing—but it didn't last any longer than it took for Nick to take Elizabeth in his arms and cover her mouth with his own. Then the teasing stopped, and the mind-blowing fireworks display that blossomed and burst behind their eyelids sent warm currents of liquid desire coursing through their veins.

Their kiss deepened, as they opened to each other, tasted each other, gloried in each other, their bodies admitting truths their minds still struggled to accept.

Nick's arms tightened around her body as Elizabeth strained closer into his embrace, her fingertips tingling as they reached up to cup his cheeks, to trace the edges of his mouth where it pressed against her own. She was as much his at that moment as she would have been if they had already consummated their love; she lived for him, breathed for him, existed only because of him.

All my life, Nick heard the chant over and over inside his head. *All my life has been lived for this, will be for this. Everything I was, everything I am or ever hope to be lies within this woman. I'm the luckiest, the most fortunate man in the world.*

They drew apart slowly, then Nick pressed his forehead against hers, his smile slow and satisfied as her eyelids came down to hide her expression, to cover her shyness at the unspoken admission they both knew she had made. ''I'll take you home now, working girl,'' he whispered quietly, kissing both her closed eyes and the tip of her nose. ''But only if you promise to have dinner with me tomorrow night.''

It was a long ride back to Spring Street, with Nicholas stopping at every corner, to lean across the midseat console to kiss Elizabeth—for Elizabeth to kiss him back.

Gammy's light was still on when they pulled up in front of the house and Elizabeth knew she wouldn't be allowed to go to bed until she had told her grandmother every last detail of her evening with Henry Lancaster, but she didn't mind. As for that strange, wonderful interlude in the garden, well, Elizabeth decided as she watched Nick's taillights disappear down the street, what her romantically minded grandmother didn't know couldn't hurt her.

Chapter Four

"Gammy, this is Nick. Nick, my grandmother—and best friend—Rose Chatham." The introductions over, Elizabeth stood back and held her breath. She never knew what her grandmother would say, and only prayed the adorable, but sometimes trying woman would behave herself.

Taking hold of Elizabeth's hand, Nick acknowledged the introduction. "Mrs. Chatham, it's a pleasure to meet you at last. Elizabeth's been keeping you under wraps for so long, I was beginning to believe you were a figment of her imagination."

"Nicholas Lancaster," Rose responded pertly, looking him over as if he were a floor lamp she might consider purchasing. "Nice. Very nice.

Sorry I missed you the other night when you came by to pick up my granddaughter, but it was my pinochle night,'' she lied easily. ''So, Nicholas Lancaster, you like children, or what?''

''Gammy! You promised me you'd behave yourself!'' Elizabeth was mortified, embarrassed beyond belief. What she wasn't, was surprised. She had purposely kept Nicholas and her grandmother apart for as long as possible, afraid something like this might happen. Now it was up to Nick, poor man, to find a way to answer her question.

Nick, luckily, had been forewarned, and as he looked down on Rose Chatham from his much greater height he produced his most ingratiating smile. ''Only if they're all as beautiful as Elizabeth, Mrs. Chatham,'' he replied, thinking his answer extremely clever.

''You want pretty boys? Well, to each his own, but I like boys to look like boys. Even John and Paul do, the little brats. And please call me Rose. Mrs. Chatham makes it sound like I'm an old lady, and if there's one thing I keep telling this family, it's that I'm not an old lady.''

''Rose it is, then,'' Nick promised, noticing that Elizabeth's facial features closely resembled her grandmother's.

''So, what are we doing standing out here in the hallway?'' Rose motioned for Elizabeth to precede her. "Everybody's around here somewhere, just waiting to get a piece of your young man, Elizabeth. We shouldn't keep them in suspense."

"Don't say I didn't warn you," Elizabeth whispered to Nick as they walked down the hallway toward the dining room, Rose following close behind them. "Now you know why I always tried to meet you at work. Leave it to my loving Gammy to open her mouth and put *my* foot in it."

"I think you were just afraid I'd take one look at your grandmother and leave you in the dirt," Nicholas whispered back. "She's wonderful."

"Hah! I heard that," Rose called after them. "Elizabeth, grab him quick, or I will. He's Henry's son, all right. Lucky for you he takes most of his looks from Katherine."

"You knew my mother?" Nick stopped abruptly at the entrance to the dining room to face Rose. "Rose Chatham, Rose Chatham," he repeated, staring at her, a puzzled expression on his face. "Wait a minute, I've got it now. You must be the Rosie my father told me about. But no, the ages wouldn't fit, would they? I mean—"

"I know what you mean, but you're wrong. I married young, and so did my son, Jack. While your father was busy building an empire, we Chathams got ourselves one generation up on him," Rose explained, enjoying herself.

"Rosie O'Hanlon! This is wonderful. Dad was wondering whatever became of you. Elizabeth, your grandmother was the one who played Cupid for my mother and father. Remember, I told you about it."

"Smart too, isn't he?" Rose quipped, feeling rather full of herself. "Elizabeth, child, what *are* you waiting for? Grab this boy!"

Nick bent down and kissed Rose on the cheek. "Thank you, Mrs. Chatham. I do think you might be the reason I'm here, if my father is to be believed. And thank you for what you just said. I have to tell you, it made my day. I guess I'll just have to keep showing Elizabeth how wonderful I am."

"My grandmother and your parents? I knew there was something, but I just didn't put it all together," Elizabeth exclaimed, looking from one to the other and praying furiously that she could change the subject. "Isn't that a coincidence. I wonder why you never told me, Gammy."

Rose turned to Elizabeth and expressively waggled her eyebrows up and down as she smiled. "No one ever tells someone else *everything*, child. Do they?"

Elizabeth flushed, her grandmother's dart hitting home. She and Nick had been dating for almost six weeks and she had shared only a small portion of what happened on those dates with Rose. "I get your point, Gammy," she admitted wryly, "but now that I've heard what Nick's father remembers, I'd love to hear the story from your side sometime."

"That goes double for me," Nick added just as Paul came around the corner from the kitchen, a stack of homemade chocolate-chip cookies in his hand.

"Hey, Nick!" he shouted familiarly, just as if Nick was a regular visitor, even though this was only his third time in the house. "Liz said you were coming over. You want to watch the Eagles game with us? Dad and John are in the den. It's just about to start."

"Elizabeth?" Nick looked at her beseechingly, just like a little boy asking his mother if it was all right to go out and play, and she laughed as she pushed him toward the den.

"Hello, Mrs. Chatham," he called out as he went past the kitchen and saw Gloria Chatham in the process of pulling a large tray of cookies out of the oven. "It certainly smells good in here."

Gloria, who had told her husband Jack just the previous evening that Nicholas Lancaster was an extremely nice young man, immediately rushed to pile ten warm cookies onto a plate and offer them to him. "Would you like milk with these or coffee, Nick?" she asked as he thanked her.

"Milk, Nick," Paul said helpfully. "They taste great dunked."

"Well, that's that," Gammy concluded once Nick and Paul had disappeared into the den to be loudly greeted with the news that the Eagles had just intercepted the kickoff on the ten-yard line. "We'll be lucky if we see them for a few minutes at halftime. Elizabeth, would you like to try your luck at a little two-handed pinochle?"

Elizabeth leaned back against the doorjamb and closed her eyes, her features glowing blissfully. "Nick fits right in here, doesn't he, Gammy? I don't know why I haven't brought him home more often," she said, sighing. "Dad likes him, Mom likes him, both the boys adore him, and Megan says he's 'boss.' Isn't it wonderful?"

Rose walked past her granddaughter to get some playing cards from the top drawer of the buffet. "Yes, dear, but I have a feeling nobody *likes* him quite as much as you do. As I seem to remember saying before, Christmas is a wonderful time for a wedding."

"Oh, Gammy, stop it," Elizabeth warned nervously. "Nick might hear you."

"So, let him," Rose goaded, sitting down at the dining-room table and beginning to expertly shuffle the cards. "Remember, I've already gotten one Lancaster man down the aisle. But, to tell you the truth, I have more confidence in this one. And from what I can see in his eyes when he looks at you, little lady, Christmas can't come too soon this year."

Central Park was trying out its brilliant fall wardrobe, the trees sporting leaves that had just begun to decorate themselves in endless colorful hues of the brightest orange and gold. The vast lawns were still lush and deeply green, while the flowers of the season winked in the warm sunlight.

As it was a Thursday, for the most part it was left to the usual horde of tourists to seek out the horse-drawn hansom cabs that were one of the more famous features of the Park. The men who drove the cabs were doing a brisk business—so brisk, in fact, that Nick was beginning to worry.

He had planned everything so carefully, so thoroughly, down to the last detail, but that didn't keep him from being extremely nervous.

He had picked Elizabeth up at her parents' home exactly at eight o'clock that morning, just in time for Jack Chatham, who had been on his way out the front door, to wink at him conspiratorially, for the two of them had had a very private, very personal discussion the night before.

Nick had presented Elizabeth with two perfectly formed long-stemmed red roses as she descended the staircase into the foyer a few minutes later, looking like a lovely wood sprite in her emerald-green wool dress and flowing beige mohair cape, and he was pleased that she had instantly realized that the flowers were meant to mark the second-month anniversary of their first meeting—their first date.

Thankfully Rose Chatham wasn't an early riser, as Jack had warned him that his mother would take one look at him and know that today was the day—the day her oldest granddaughter would become engaged. ''Not that I don't think she figured it out the minute she heard you were taking Liz to New York, but I do think it'll be easier if you don't have to try to keep a straight face while she's winking at you and throwing out hints to Liz,'' Jack had commented as he handed Nick a glass of beer to toast the conclusion of their discussion.

The chauffeur-driven Rolls-Royce he'd hired on a whim had smoothly whisked Nick and Elizabeth out of Bethlehem while they nibbled on flaky croissants, sipped good champagne and giggled like guilty children in the wide midnight-blue velvet back seat. They drove smoothly across the state line out of Pennsylvania and onto the New Jersey

Turnpike, then through the Lincoln Tunnel and into New York City.

The mild November weather was cooperating beautifully, just as the morning weatherman had promised three days earlier while Nick lay in bed in his apartment, drinking his second cup of coffee and hatching his plan. It was a beautiful plan, close to a divine inspiration, he had decided modestly, and he'd been on pins and needles ever since, feeling as if Thursday would never come.

Once in the city, Nick had dismissed the driver and then strolled hand in hand with Elizabeth through the Park for an hour before they adjourned to Tavern on the Green to share a leisurely lunch in the restaurant's famous Crystal Room.

Nick knew Elizabeth had enjoyed their lunch thoroughly, for her warm brown eyes had shone with almost childlike delight as she had exclaimed over the multicolored chandeliers and the huge, succulent shrimp while smiling at the small army of waiters that had eagerly anticipated her every wish.

He had gloried in her excitement, pleased that she was pleased, and privately congratulated himself for having been the architect of her pleasure.

"I feel like a queen," she had told him after thanking Bruce, one of their waiters, for refilling her nearly full water goblet for the third time.

"You never cease to amaze me, Nicholas Lancaster. Just imagine, driving all the way into New York just to have lunch. And that champagne! I've never had champagne before noon in my entire life. Anyone would think this was some really special occasion."

But it is a special occasion, Nick thought nervously now that they were back out on the sidewalk, leaning his dark head forward to see if one of the cabs was on its way back to the waiting area. *This is probably the second most special occasion in my life, with the first yet to come. Damn it, why didn't I think to reserve a cab? Sloppy, Lancaster, sloppy. It just goes to show what falling in love can do to a man's brain. Who in hell could know everybody and their brother would pick today to take a spin around the Park?*

"We don't have to take a ride, Nick," Elizabeth told him, lightly touching his sleeve to get his attention. "Really, I'd be just as happy if we walked. I've eaten so much it would probably do me good. Bruce said they're filming a movie somewhere around here—some sort of police chase story. Maybe we can watch."

"No!" Nick exclaimed hastily. Too hastily, he realized as Elizabeth looked up at him questioningly. "That is, I really do want to ride in one of those carriages. I never have, you know. Please, darling, indulge me a little. Let's play the tourist all the way.''

Elizabeth raised herself onto her toes and kissed his cheek, her joy at being with him making her silly. "Only if you promise to take me to the top of the Empire State Building afterward, Daddy—please, please?''

"Smart aleck," Nick answered, giving the tip of her nose a light flick with his finger.

The cab that eventually pulled up in front of them was one of the newer ones, all red leather and shiny black paint. There was even a huge white horse sporting a hot-pink feather headdress as he stood quietly between the shafts, and a brash young Irishman was perched on the seat, a white cockade tucked in the band of his bowler hat.

The fact that the driver was also wearing faded designer jeans and a blue sweatshirt that said Let's Go Mets couldn't dampen Nick's excitement as he helped Elizabeth up onto the soft leather seat.

"Oh, Nick, this is wonderful." Elizabeth sighed in delight, snuggling into the seat. "I feel like I should bow my head and wave to the passersby, like Princess Di.''

Nick smiled at her and shook his head. *It's happening, it's finally happening,* was all he could think, swallowing hard, like a nervous schoolboy about to ask the head cheerleader to the junior prom. "Once around the Park, please, and take your time," Nick commanded tersely, knowing his request sounded like a cliché. He slipped the driver a healthy tip, almost as an apology.

"And what else would you be wantin', I wonder, what with a fine beauty like this dear lady here up beside you?" the young man quipped cheekily, throwing Elizabeth a broad wink.

"Isn't he sweet?" Elizabeth whispered confidentially as Nick gingerly lowered his long, lean frame onto the seat beside her. "I can't understand why anyone thinks New Yorkers are cold. I've always found them to be very friendly, and almost all of them seem to be from somewhere else. It's almost as if New York is several dozen small towns all strung together on the same string, like multicolored beads. While I was living here I met dozens of really lovely people from different areas of Pennsylvania's coal regions."

"You shouldn't talk to strangers, Elizabeth," Nick felt he had to remind her, having learned that, to Elizabeth, strangers were only friends she hadn't yet met. Hadn't she been friendly to him after he had crashed into her that first day? Her openness, her friendliness, was just one of the many things he loved about her.

"Yes, darling," she replied evenly, and he knew she was only agreeing with him to be polite. "You know, Nick, for all the time I lived here, I never went for one of these rides. You're spoiling me, darling, and I love you for it!''

Nick felt his heart do a small flip in his chest as Elizabeth turned her glowing face up to his, her thick, chin-length, sweet-smelling chestnut hair dancing in the slight breeze so that it lightly caressed his cheek as she resettled herself within the circle of his arm. He kissed the tip of her nose as the driver moved the cab away from the curb. *She loves me for that. Please, Lord, let her mean it.*

''It's easy to spoil you, Elizabeth,'' he assured her, checking his suit pocket for the tenth time in ten minutes, just to be sure the small package was still safely tucked inside. He took a deep breath and tried to relax, looking at Elizabeth out of the corner of his eye.

She was beautiful; small, perfectly formed to fit in his arms, and he felt all-powerful, responsible for her in a way that brought out a tenderness he had never guessed he possessed. *And I'm about to make my possession official!*

She sat beside him, her sun-kissed face animated as she eagerly took in the sights and sounds of the Park, her hands unconsciously twirling the huge yellow-centered daisy he had bought for her from a strolling flower seller, and he leaned his head back to bathe his own face in the warm sunshine, reliving their first explosive meeting.

In his thirty-two years, Nick could not recall another example of the instant compatability he and Elizabeth had shared, or his intense need to see her, touch her, hold her, that had been with him ever since. If he had been right in his first assumption, if he was a victim of love at first sight, he would go happily to his fate.

His feelings for her were physical, he knew—had known from the beginning—intensely so, but they weren't limited to his barely hidden desire to take her to his bed. She appealed to his mind, to his heart, to his recently surfaced desire to make a home, to father a whole brood of chestnut-haired children with huge, laughing brown eyes. Being with Elizabeth had been a mixture of heaven and hell, and even now he wondered why it had taken him so long to ask her to be his wife.

He patted his suit pocket yet again, closed his eyes and reveled in the warm, satisfying feeling that had invaded his chest. This was right, this was so perfectly, so wonderfully right.

Elizabeth closed her eyes and tried to hold back an inane grin. Everything was perfect, completely, absolutely and deliciously perfect. The Park, the weather, the hansom cab—and most especially, the man by her side. *Gammy will go crazy when I tell her about this cab ride!*

She supposed she may have spent happier days in her twenty-six years, but at the moment she couldn't remember a single one. Nothing could compare to the absolute perfection of this day, not even the Christmas when she was eleven and had gotten that fire-engine red two-wheel bike with the white wicker basket and the shiny silver bell on the handlebar. It was a silly example, she knew, but then she was feeling silly. Silly and light-hearted—and maybe even a little light-headed.

Nothing in her experience had prepared Elizabeth for Nicholas Lancaster, and she still couldn't decide if he was everything she had ever wanted, or only a dream that was too good to be true.

The past two months had blended into one long roller-coaster ride. The times she and Nick had spent together were the exciting, dizzying climbs to the top of the highest hills, the hours they were apart the small valleys between, passing by too quickly to allow her to catch her breath, but lasting just long enough to build her desire to be catapulted up the next steep incline and embrace the delicious excitement of seeing what lay on the other side.

She snuggled more closely against Nick's shoulder as the cabdriver urged his horse onto the street alongside the Park. She pretended to be chilly so that his cashmere-tweed-covered arm would automatically tighten around her.

Elizabeth felt so safe with Nick, so cosseted. Yet she was always aware of the strong sensual undercurrent that ran between them, the desire to be one with each other, to belong to each other totally, in every way there was. She knew Nick wanted her, and loved him even more for not pressing her to give herself to him—behaving just the way her grandmother had always told her honorable men did with the women they really loved.

And their physical attraction had been there since the beginning, she thought now, since the first moment she had impulsively reached out to comfort him after they had collided in the housewares department. Elizabeth felt herself blushing as she remembered how she had babbled, saying anything and everything that had come into her head, trying to cover her nervousness. But Nick had felt it, too; he must have, because he had asked her out for lunch.

And dinner that night, and the next night, and the next—and the next. She rubbed her cheek against his jacket as she remembered her grandmother's prediction that she, Elizabeth Anne Chatham, was meant to marry Nicholas Lancaster.

And that was after our first date! Dear Gammy,

she thinks its wonderful, like something out of those old Hollywood movies. I think she even believes she had something to do with our coming together. She certainly was acting strange last night when she made me leave Nick and come upstairs to help her find her eyeglasses—especially when we finally found them in the kitchen. I just hate it when she knows something I don't know.

"Warm enough, darling?" Nick asked, breaking in on her thoughts just as she felt a shiver of hopeful anticipation run down her spine.

Could Nick have said something to Gammy? Or to Dad, once the two of them were alone? They weren't acting suspicious, or were they? Could Nick be planning something for today—something like—oh, no, it's just too ridiculous. He couldn't be, could he? Elizabeth looked up at Nick searchingly, but his eyes were clear and unclouded.

She berated herself for her wild imagination and tried to tell herself she wasn't disappointed. Did she really think he was going to propose? It was silly. She'd only known him for two months. People didn't propose after knowing someone for only two months. *Did they?*

"Uh, no, I'm fine," she said in a rush as Nick's eyebrows came together in a frown. "I'm just enjoying the ride."

"Good," Nick answered, and she knew he was

wondering what was wrong with her, why she looked and sounded so frightened.

She snuggled back against his shoulder once more and surrendered to her daydream, picturing Nick's face as he asked her to marry him. *Oh, how I love this man. He's so sweet, so thoughtful—so wonderfully romantic! I believe I could ride like this forever—into the sunset, my dearest love, and I...*

Nick patted his suit pocket again, cleared his throat, and called Elizabeth's attention to the large crowd standing near a barricaded side street. "Look over there, Elizabeth, I think that might be where they're doing the filming your friend the waiter told us about."

"That it 'tis, sir, right enough," the driver piped up informatively, also looking toward the side street. "It's for a television show, you know, the one where that fella with the fancy sports car sticks up for the little guy?"

"Oh, I watch that show all the time!" Elizabeth exclaimed, eagerly leaning toward the left side of the cab to watch until they had moved past the alleyway, and giving Nick the time he needed to slip the small package out of his pocket and conceal it in his fist. "I think Megan's half in love with the hero, although she'd probably strangle me if she knew I told you, Nick. She's going through a phase, I think, and says television is a complete waste. This from a girl who practically grew up in front of the boob tube. Nick? What are you doing?''

''My shoelace has come undone somehow,'' Nick answered quickly, hiding his smile as he leaned down to retie the lace he had purposely loosened earlier, then placed the package carefully on the floor of the cab near Elizabeth's feet. It wasn't the most original idea he'd ever had, but somehow, considering the way they had met, it seemed to fit the situation.

He sat back on the seat, then fumbled in his pockets. ''Damn, I must have dropped it.''

''Dropped what?'' Elizabeth asked as if on cue, already leaning forward to search the floor of the cab for whatever it was Nick had lost. ''I don't see anything—oh heavens, what's this?''

''What's what?''

She sat up slowly, holding the small, square silver-wrapped package gingerly with both hands, eyeing it warily, as if it were alive and might bite her. ''This. It's a box. It's got a bow on it,'' she said, swallowing hard. *Oh, please let this be a ring. Please, let me be right!*

Nick closed his eyes for a moment, knowing he was scared. Not a little nervous, not slightly apprehensive, but downright wet palms, dry mouth scared. What if he had read the signals all wrong? What if Jack Chatham had only been polite? What if Elizabeth didn't want him? What if she lived for her career and had no plans to marry before she was thirty-five? What if she hated him? What if— oh, how had he ever come up with such a stupid idea? He was a grown man, for God's sake, and here he was, shaking like a kid on his first date.

"I—I guess I should open it," Elizabeth stammered, her hands shaking so badly she couldn't loosen the bow. *It's probably a pair of diamond earrings. Men like to give earrings. Oh, please, don't let it be earrings!*

"All right," Nick agreed as casually as he could, swallowing hard and putting his arm around her tentatively. This was it; this was the moment he had been waiting for, working toward, plotting out so meticulously. "If you want to."

Elizabeth made a few more attempts, barely able to see through the tears she was sure he'd notice, until at last she gave up and thrust the box into his lap. "Oh, this is just impossible! Here, you open it for me, Nick! I'm shaking too hard."

Nick shook his head, laughing silently, suddenly not quite as nervous as he had been. Leave it to Elizabeth to turn the simply tied bow into a tangled knot. Her mechanical ineptitude was only one of the many things about her that delighted him. He quickly untied the bow while keeping Elizabeth firmly inside his embrace, then handed her the box, watching as she removed the silver wrapping and lifted the lid.

"Oh, dear," Elizabeth squeaked, tipping the brown velvet case into her hand, Nick's soft breath warming her cheek. He pressed his head close to hers while she slowly pushed up the lid to expose the contents.

It is, it is, it is! Oh, Gammy, you were right, you were so right. He loves me, Nick really does love me! Oh, no, I'm going to cry! Her first tears fell onto the velvet padding surrounding the perfectly formed marquise diamond that twinkled with blue fire between matching rows of baguettes, the whole encased in a thin circle of gold.

"It—it's beautiful," she whispered almost reverently. Her tears were falling freely now, and her full lower lip trembled as she said, "It's the most beautiful thing I've ever seen." *Oh, please, Lord, don't let me be dreaming!*

"And that makes you cry?" *It's all right, darling,* he thought to himself. *I think I feel like crying, too.*

"I'm not crying."

"Yes, darling, you are. Very prettily, but crying

just the same.'' *It's all right, everything's all right. She loves me!*

Elizabeth's hand reached up and touched her wet cheeks. "Oh, dear, I am crying. I'm sorry. This is for me, isn't it? Please tell me it's not just something someone lost in the cab? I think I'd die if—''

Nick relaxed completely, at last. Reaching for the ring and her nervously shaking left hand, he then slipped the diamond onto her finger. It was a perfect fit. Raising her hand to his lips, he stared deeply into her eyes, knowing that no words could possibly add to the perfection of the moment. Then he placed a soft kiss just where the ring encircled her finger.

Elizabeth watched, fascinated, her head tipped to one side, her gaze tender, as Nick's warm lips lingered on her tingling fingers. She felt her body instinctively melting in his direction. "Oh, Nick," she breathed, oblivious to everything except what was happening to them, between them, in the snug cocoon of the New York City hansom cab as the white horse carried them back through the gate into Central Park.

At last Nick, his voice husky with emotion, asked, "You will marry me, Elizabeth, won't you? I love you, darling. I love you very, very much."

Her answer was breathed into his mouth as she

gave herself up to his embrace, just as the cab drew up alongside the curb in front of the restaurant.

The driver peeked back over his shoulder, then flicked the reins to set the cab in motion again. "Once more around the Park, Maureen, m'love. And this one's on the house!"

Chapter Five

"So, now the fun starts!"

Elizabeth didn't know quite what she had expected her grandmother to say when she and Nick showed her the engagement ring, perhaps something like "I told you so," but Rose Chatham had surprised her again. "Fun, Gammy? What do you mean?"

Although she was disappointed that no one else was at home when they returned from New York just before dark, Elizabeth was glad that the three of them were going to have some time together to talk about the day. Besides, if this was the response she was going to get from her grandmother, maybe it would be easier on Nick if the Chatham clan voiced their opinions one at a time.

"Yes, dear, you heard me—fun!" Rose repeated, clapping her hands in glee. She went up to Elizabeth and Nick, took them each by the hand and led them to the living room. "Hurry, we don't have much time before everyone comes home from John's basketball game and this place turns into a three-ring circus. Now, come, my children, and you'll hear just what I mean. Nick, my dear, you will indulge me, won't you?"

"Do I have a choice?" As they were dragged along behind the little woman, Nick winked at Elizabeth, clearly enjoying himself. "I hoped your grandmother would be happy about this, but I think I may have underestimated her. She's really thrilled, isn't she?"

Overhearing him, Rose shot back happily, "You bet I'm thrilled! Nicholas, I've been planning for this since the day this child was born. So, no, you don't have any choice, unless you want me to tell your father on you. Now sit down, here, on either side of me and listen. You do want a nice wedding, don't you, Elizabeth?"

The three of them sat on the bright green floral slip-covered couch, Rose still not releasing their hands. Elizabeth lowered her head, avoiding Nick's eyes as she answered her grandmother's question. "Well, to tell you the truth, Gammy, I have thought about the sort of wedding I'd like;

every girl does, I imagine. I think I'd like it to be old-fashioned—traditional—oh, you know what I mean. But—"

"But nothing! That's exactly what I want, too, with a nuptial mass, and a long veil, and your cousin Bill singing 'Ave Maria' as you give flowers to the Blessed Mother. I'm going to bawl like a baby through the whole thing, and enjoy every wonderful minute of it. You're going to be the most beautiful bride, Elizabeth. Isn't she, Nick?"

"Absolutely beautiful," he agreed, leaning forward around Rose to smile at his fiancée of six hours. Nick didn't know what else to say. When he had thought about the future it had only included Elizabeth and himself and a home of their own, a place where they could be alone together with their love. Then, a little later, the children would come, to make their family complete.

That's what marriage meant to Nick. A wedding was nothing more than the necessary ceremony that would officially join them together. He couldn't have cared less about anything but getting it over with as quickly and as painlessly as possible. But, obviously, there were certain things about marriage that he hadn't considered, and his confused expression made that very clear.

Rose threw back her head and laughed with delight at Nick's discomfort. "He doesn't have the faintest idea what I'm talking about, Elizabeth! Isn't that just like a man? You would like to get married tomorrow, isn't that right, Nick—or even tonight? Well, I can tell you, it isn't that easy. There are plans to be made, the church to be reserved, flowers to be ordered, a gown to be bought—oh, a million lovely things to do.''

Elizabeth suddenly felt uneasy. Rose's plans sounded so exciting, so much like the dreams she'd had herself as a young girl, but she would have to be blind not to see that Nick was looking somewhat harassed. ''Really, Gammy, I don't see any real need to go to all this fuss. It's not like we're children, after all. I think we might be past the shoes and rice sort of thing. I'm sure a very small, quiet ceremony would do just as well.''

Rose sank back against the couch cushions like a small rag doll whose stuffing had been knocked out, her bottom lip forming a petulant pout. ''You're no fun, Elizabeth Anne, no fun at all. And you, Nicholas,'' she went on, turning her head toward him and impaling him with her steely gaze, ''do you really want to marry Elizabeth in some tawdry hole-and-corner affair? What would your father say?''

''I hardly think I'd involve Elizabeth in anything tawdry, Mrs. Chatham,'' Nick replied, trying hard not to laugh. Elizabeth's grandmother looked about as menacing as a fluffy kitten, but he'd say one thing for her—she certainly knew where to apply her claws.

"Of course you wouldn't, Nick," she agreed, patting his arm. "And please, now that we're going to be family, call me Rose. Now, are you going to let Elizabeth miss the best day of her life just because you're in a hurry? I mean, I can't imagine you'd be just as happy to bop her on the head, throw her over your shoulder and carry her off to your cave, now would you?"

"Oh, Gammy, please don't throw a tantrum," Elizabeth warned, wondering if Nick would ask her to return the ring, believing insanity ran in the family.

But Nick wasn't insulted; he was thinking about his father, about the man's great love of ceremony, about the many times he had heard Henry Lancaster speak of his own wedding day, and the pride he'd felt when his own bride had walked down the aisle to meet him. Would Nick regret it for the rest of his life if he denied himself the same sort of wonderful memory? If he, through his own impatience, denied Elizabeth the day she deserved?

"Rose," he said at last, taking her hands, "my bride is going to be the most beautiful bride that ever walked down an aisle, and her wedding day is going to be perfect, in every way. I don't know where my mind was to even think about a small, quick ceremony. Thank goodness you're here. Please, can we count on your advice?''

''Oh, brother, here we go. Hold on to your hats everybody,'' Elizabeth grumbled good-naturedly, knowing that yet another man had succumbed to her irrepressible, irascible grandmother and her Irish wiles. Thanks to Nick's well-meaning politeness, they had just relinquished all control over whatever would happen to them between now and their wedding day.

Immediately—after having gotten her own way, as she had been sure all along that she would—Rose was all business. ''All right, children! Now you're talking. Elizabeth, Nick, what do you think about a Christmas wedding? Poinsettias on the altar, either white ones or red, I'm not sure yet which it should be—maybe both—and candles, lots of candles. And white bows on the ends of the pews, of course, and, Elizabeth, you should have a cathedral-length train, it's so elegant. We'll have to hurry, of course, as it takes so long for gowns to be ordered. We're going to have to hope you can wear one of the gowns the store has in stock.''

''A gown,'' Elizabeth repeated wondrously, suddenly misty-eyed in spite of her misgivings. ''Yes, I think I can see it. Something with a full skirt that rustles when I walk, and a train that bustles up for dancing. We'll go Saturday, Gammy, if it's all right with you and Mother.''

"That's my girl! Gloria will cry the whole day long. Won't it be grand? Now, for the bridesmaids. You'll have Megan, naturally, and that friend of yours from New York. What's her name? Beth, isn't it? Yes, of course. Such a pretty girl, all that lovely blond hair. Wait till you meet her, Nick, she has the loveliest speaking voice, all soft and breathy. And for your matron of honor, Jennifer; she's a redhead, isn't she?''

"I think I'd like to have Lisa as one of the bridesmaids," Elizabeth slipped in, remembering the good times she and her cousin had had together during their teens, when Lisa had visited during the summer vacations.

"Yes, yes, I was just coming to Lisa. She has black hair, and your high-school friends, Nora, Lorraine, and Rosemary, they all have brown—my goodness, that's quite a mix. We'll have to be very careful of the colors when we choose their gowns. Nick, you do have five friends for ushers, don't you? You'll want John and Paul for the other two; I can blackmail them into behaving themselves.''

"Fourteen attendants?" Nick said, quickly totaling the number on his fingers. He could feel his control of the situation rapidly slipping away.

"Yes, yes, not counting the ring bearers. Your

cousin Bonnie's boys are just the right age, Elizabeth. Have you thought of a best man yet, Nick? Oh, dear, let me get a pen and paper. We'll have to start making lists.'' She impulsively kissed each of them on the cheek as she clambered to her feet. ''Oh, this is going to be *such fun*!''

Nick stood as Rose scurried out of the room, then sat down, cupped his chin in his hand, turned his head to the side to look at Elizabeth and sighed. ''I think I'm getting a headache. You know, darling, it's a good thing I only plan to go through this once.''

Elizabeth smiled and scooted over to slide her arms around his neck. ''I told you Gammy was a handful, and you, my poor darling, were like putty in her hands. But honestly, Nick, we don't have to go the whole nine yards if you don't want to. I'll understand.''

Nick took hold of her shoulders and looked down at her face, his heart in his eyes. ''Rose is right. Besides, Christmas isn't that far away. You'd be surprised how hardheaded I could have gotten if she had started making noises about a June wedding. You're going to make a beautiful bride, Elizabeth soon-to-be Lancaster. And I wouldn't miss it for the world.''

''Oh, Nick,'' Elizabeth said on a relieved sigh

as she sought his mouth with her own. "I do love you. I love you so very, very much!"

"This is wonderful news! Come in, come in, and sit down over here. What do you mean, is it too late? Are you calling me an old man, Nicholas?"

It was almost ten, his father's usual bedtime, but it had taken some time to extract Elizabeth from her family once they had all come home, and even now their congratulations were ringing in his ears. The news could have waited for the morning, Nick knew, but Elizabeth had insisted that it would only be fair to tell both families the same day.

Now he was glad they hadn't waited. Nick couldn't remember the last time he had seen his father this happy. Ever since he had bumped himself up to chairman of the board, Henry had spent less and less time at the store and devoted more of his life to the garden that had been his wife's greatest passion. He was getting older, Henry had complained, and Nick had secretly agreed that his father was beginning to show his years.

Yet as Elizabeth and Nick sat with him in the living room of his home, Henry looked ten years younger. After shaking Nick's hands vigorously and giving Elizabeth kisses on both cheeks, he had immediately gotten down to the business of the wedding, reminding Nick of Rose Chatham's re-action to their news.

Once Mrs. Gillespie had offered her own best wishes and served champagne—a bottle Henry had chosen the night he'd first met Elizabeth, already anticipating this occasion—he announced, "I won't say this is sudden, son, because I could tell when I first met her that Elizabeth here was the woman for you. She's so like your mother, her gentleness shows in her every movement. My dear, have you given any thought to what sort of wed-ding you'll want?"

Nick leaned over to whisper in Elizabeth's ear. "Here we go again. Why do I get the sinking feel-ing that when it comes to weddings, the groom is only a convenient warm body to hang the bride on?"

Elizabeth knew Nick was joking, but she also knew he had a point. Everyone was behaving most peculiarly. Her grandmother had barely stopped talking to come up for air all evening, and she even had Elizabeth almost believing that there was noth-ing else happening in the world that held a candle to the upcoming wedding. Nick, at least to her grandmother's way of thinking, had performed his single function—he had proposed.

When the family had come home, Megan had immediately wanted to know if each bridesmaid would have her own limousine, and put the entire family on notice that she'd rather walk down the aisle bald than be partnered with either of her brothers. Not only that, but she had made known her preference for a green gown—"to match the season, silly"—while Elizabeth knew that her friend Beth never wore green because she thought it made her complexion look sallow.

Paul and John, not known for their tact, had quickly tired of the talk of the wedding and could be overheard in the kitchen conspiring to paint Help me! on the soles of Nick's shoes, a prank that they were sure would have the guests rolling in the aisle the first time the groom knelt at the altar. Nick was the only one who thought that that was funny, she remembered now, looking at him strangely.

Jack Chatham, Elizabeth's father, normally a quiet man who cheerfully left the everyday running of the household to the women of the family, had then announced firmly that he planned to hire his lifelong friend, Jimmy Timenski, leader of a local group called Jimmy Timenski and His Polka Dots, to play at the reception.

"Dad, no!" Megan had groaned, dramatically flinging herself onto the couch. "Not accordions! I'll die, I mean I'll absolutely *perish* from embarrassment."

In Elizabeth's mind, the only sane person left in

the family was her mother. After she had dried her tears of happiness, Gloria Chatham had immediately gotten busy formulating a list of all the relatives who would be happy to assist in the baking that would probably go on for weeks preceding the ceremony, so that the reception afterward in the church's all-purpose hall would be overflowing with nut rolls, miniature cakes and apricot kiffle pastries—a particular favorite of the Chatham side of the family.

"Well, actually," Elizabeth admitted now, realizing that Henry Lancaster was waiting for her answer, "my family has surprised me by having quite a few rather definite plans for the wedding."

"Especially her grandmother," Nick put in. "Talk about your 'idea' people—that woman missed her calling. Rose should have been a general. She could probably plan a major campaign, outfit a battle battalion from boots to tanks and have it on its way in ten minutes."

"Rosie O'Hanlon," Henry said, smiling at the mental picture the name drew for him. "She came no higher than my shoulder, as I remember, but she made you feel as if she were ten feet tall. Elizabeth, ever since Nick told me who your grandmother is, I've been anxious to see her again. Indeed, as father of the groom, I believe I remember that it's up to me to have your parents here to dinner as soon as possible. Naturally that invitation will include Rosie. Let me know your phone number, my dear, and I'll give them a call tomorrow morning.''

''That's very kind of you. I'm sure Gammy and my parents will be delighted,'' Elizabeth told him, privately grateful Nick's father hadn't included the other three Chatham children in the invitation. Not that she was ashamed of her siblings, for she wasn't, but things were moving too quickly for her to believe that having Megan, John and Paul in on a discussion of the wedding plans at this stage of the game would do anything but confuse the issue.

''Mrs. Chatham—Rose, that is—would like us to have a Christmas wedding, Dad,'' Nick said, bringing the discussion back to the ceremony itself. ''What do you think?''

''Christmas?'' Henry repeated. ''I imagine you mean the day after Christmas?''

Elizabeth nodded. ''Gammy wanted it to be Christmas Day, but that's really a difficult day. I think the day after Christmas is perfect. Unless it snows,'' she added quietly, frowning at the thought.

Henry reached into a nearby drawer and pulled out a small calendar, counting off the weeks until the holiday. ''That's rather short notice, isn't it? I mean, I'll have to see if the club's available, for one thing. It will probably be closed, but I think I can pull a few strings—cost is no object. And then there's the orchestra to consider. Nick, what was the name of that orchestra they had at the club for the Governor's Ball last spring?''

Nick shifted uncomfortably in his seat, not unaware of Elizabeth's sharp intake of breath. ''Richard Burrows and his Orchestra,'' he said automatically before continuing: ''Look, Dad, I think you should know that Mr. and Mrs. Chatham have already begun discussing the reception and the orchestra. You wouldn't want to commit us to anything without first talking it over with them. After all, I really think the bride's family is responsible for such things. Isn't that right, darling?'' he ended, looking toward Elizabeth, who could have cheerfully strangled him for putting her in the position of answering such an obviously leading question.

''Well, traditionally, yes, I think so,'' she replied, unconsciously seeking Nick's hand and squeezing it tightly. ''But I was in my friend Jennifer's wedding last year, and I know that the etiquette has changed over the years, so that the financial burden is no longer entirely with the bride's family. As a matter of fact, today more and more couples are paying for their own weddings.''

''Nonsense!'' Henry exclaimed, rising to his

feet. "I never heard of such a thing. Oh, how I wish Katherine was here. She'd know just what to do. Elizabeth, I'm going to call Rosie tomorrow morning and we'll get this whole thing straightened out. Pay for the wedding yourselves? Not while there's breath in my body you won't."

Now it was Nick's turn to stand. "Dad, I think you're forgetting something. Elizabeth has a mother and father. I know you and Elizabeth's grandmother go back a long way, but I don't think it would be wise to go over their heads. Besides, both Elizabeth and I have good jobs. I think we should pay for the wedding ourselves. I haven't asked you for money since I was fourteen and got my own paper route."

Elizabeth looked from one man to the other, seeing as well as sensing that a sudden battle of wills was about to take place in front of her. Rising quickly, she stepped between them to give Henry Lancaster another kiss. "I'll tell Gammy you're going to call her, Mr. Lancaster. I know she'll be delighted. And on my lunch hour tomorrow I'll go to the bookstore and buy an armful of bridal magazines and etiquette manuals. But until then, to be perfectly honest with you, I think I'm just so happy that Nick and I are going to be married that I really can't think of anything else. Everything's happening so fast. Why, we just got engaged this afternoon. Isn't that right, darling?''

"Like I said, son,'' Henry replied, chuckling, "she reminds me of your mother. A born diplomat. But I have to agree with Elizabeth. Rosie and I will have lunch as soon as possible, just to talk over old times, and she and Elizabeth's parents will come to dinner Saturday night if they're free. We'll put our heads together then. I want to do this thing right.''

"I don't want to say good-night.''

Elizabeth slid her hands down Nick's arms so that they stood facing each other, their hands clasped together at their sides as they stared into each other's eyes. "I don't want to say good-night, either.''

It was past midnight as they stood on the Chatham front porch, reluctant to let this special day end. After leaving Henry Lancaster's house Nick had driven around Bethlehem, the two of them remarking that every year the Christmas decorations were going up earlier on the city streets. They had stopped at a small restaurant for a light snack that neither of them ate, and afterward walked hand in hand down Broad Street, looking at the displays in the shop windows.

But they both had to go to work in the morning

and it had been a long day, so that at last Nick had reluctantly driven back to the house on Spring Street. They had been standing together on the porch ever since, still finding it impossible to say good-night and part from each other.

They were engaged now, promised to each other, and it seemed unfair that they should have to go home separately, to lie in their lonely beds and only dream of the day when they would be able to say good-night and never have to part again.

Nick had kissed Elizabeth good-night three times; and three times he had made it only as far as the first step of the porch before coming back to take her in his arms once again. "This is crazy," he said now as he drew her body against his and buried his face in her hair. "I think it would be easier to rip my heart out than to walk away and leave you here. Elizabeth, darling, I don't know if I can go through with this. I want us to be married—now."

Elizabeth felt tears gathering in the corners of her eyes even as she gloried in the slight shuddering of Nick's body as he clasped her tightly to his chest. She knew how he felt because she was feeling the same way. They belonged together, and waiting for Christmas to come this year would be the hardest thing she had ever done.

"I know, darling, I know," she assured him, nuzzling her cheek against the front of his coat. "I just want to run off somewhere private and hold you forever. This is silly; we're mature adults. After all, it's not like we won't be seeing each other tomorrow. Why are we feeling this way?"

Suddenly Nick smiled. "I can think of one reason. *Grrrr,*" he growled, nibbling at the side of her throat. "Like you said, we're all grown up, aren't we?"

"Nicholas Lancaster, shame on you!" Elizabeth reprimanded, feigning shock. "My mother warned me about boys like you. Lucky for you that your intentions are honorable, or I'd have to scream for my father so that he could toss you down the porch steps on your head."

Moving his lips from her throat to her ear, Nick warned: "Better start yelling, darling, because at the moment my intentions don't have a whole hell of a lot to do with honor. I'm a desperate man, Elizabeth. Now stop talking and give me your mouth."

The porch light flicked on and off three times, stopping Nick just as Elizabeth had turned her face to his, obedient to his playful demand. "Gammy," she acknowledged, sighing. "I think she's trying in her own inimitable way to tell us to stop putting on a show for the neighbors."

"Tell her we'll sell tickets and give her ten percent off the top," Nick said, still intent on getting his own way.

"Nicholas," Elizabeth scolded, giving him one last quick kiss before reluctantly pulling free of his arms, "I'd better go in now, before Gammy decides to come out here on the porch to share her latest brainstorm with us. I wouldn't put it past her, you know."

Nick laughed as he remembered his last sight of Rose as the woman paced up and down the dining room spouting random ideas for the wedding. "Neither would I. All right, darling, I'll go quietly. Just remember—I love you. I love you madly... and passionately...and wildly..." he said, kissing her to punctuate each word "...and eternally... and—dammit!"

The light flicked on and off three more times as Elizabeth collapsed against Nick with a fit of giggles. "Mrs. Williamson across the street must be standing at her window with her binoculars again. Gammy says it's her only pleasure in life, spying on us Chathams."

"That's not funny!" he pointed out, but he looked across the street anyway, just in time to see a lace curtain on the second floor of the corner house sliding back into place. "Like I seem to remember saying before," he said as he backed down the porch steps, "Christmas can't come too soon this year!"

"Good night, darling!" Elizabeth called after him, waving until he started the engine and switched on his headlights, and then finally turning to put her hand on the doorknob. Just as her fingers connected with the doorknob the door flew inward and she was catapulted into the foyer, to see her grandmother standing on the other side of the door.

"Finally! I thought he'd never leave! That old biddy Williamson will be hanging over the back fence all day tomorrow talking about you, young lady. I can't wait to tell her about that rock on your finger. Talk about taking the wind out of somebody's sails. Well, don't just stand there gaping at me, come up to my room. We have so much to talk about."

Elizabeth leaned down and kissed her grandmother's cheek. "We're in love, Gammy," she gushed happily. "Isn't it wonderful?"

Rose looked at her granddaughter, saw the dreamy glow in her eyes and groaned. "Go to bed, Elizabeth. I know when I'm licked. We'll talk in the morning."

Chapter Six

Life, Elizabeth decided while putting a stack of just-completed order sheets into her Out basket, and feeling a giddy thrill go through her as her ring caught the light and became a glittering burst of color, was actually rather wonderful.

She was engaged to be married. That, all by itself, was the fulfillment of a dream. She had always suspected that she wasn't cut out for the dog-eat-dog world of business, and her three years in New York after graduating from Moravian College had taught her that, for her, a career wasn't the be-all and end-all of her existence.

After all, wasn't that exactly why she had come back to Bethlehem in the first place? She had missed her home, had missed her family and she was ready to settle down. Her grandmother's teasing had been right on target; she was ready for marriage.

Using her parents' happy marriage, and her grandmother's stories of her own married life as models, Elizabeth had grown up with a healthy regard for the rightness of the institution, and she had never had any problem seeing herself in the role of traditional wife and mother. She was, she concluded happily, just an old-fashioned sort of female.

But now the reality that she had found with Nick had far surpassed even her wildest dreams. Marriage itself had become secondary; it was the man and the man alone who counted. If Nick had not become the reason for her existence, he certainly had given that existence real meaning. She had known from the moment he'd first touched her hand that he was different, special; but almost overnight he had become the most important person in her life.

Sitting back in her chair, Elizabeth hugged herself tightly to keep from crying out with happiness. Here, in the small office behind the housewares department, she felt as if she would burst into song at any moment. She could dance, she could float on air. Love was the most wonderful, the most lovely emotion in the entire world.

It had nothing to do with curtains on windows or freshly baked brownies cooling on top of the stove. Love, she concluded, had to do with finding that one special person in the entire world who had the power to make you want to have it all, even as you were giving it all away with both hands. The house they would live in, the children they would have, these were all lovely to think about, to discuss, to weave dreams around. But without that one special man, they meant nothing.

She was so lucky, she decided, so very, very lucky. Thousands of people, maybe even millions, lived their entire lives without ever finding that one special person. Why if she had decided to stay in New York, she never would have met Nick at all.

Elizabeth shivered at the thought. Never to have met Nick? Never to have known his love? It was unthinkable. She shook her head, dismissing such an unsettling thought. She *had* met him. They *had* fallen in love. And in just five more weeks, they *would* be man and wife, never to be separated again. Yes, life was wonderful!

"Miss Chatham, the Reading store is on line one," Judy Holland said, poking her head into the office and politely not commenting on the idiotically blissful expression on her boss's face.

"Something about a shipment of Christmas tree cookie cutters being lost somewhere in transit. Shall I tell them you'll call back?"

"No, thank you, Judy, I'll take it in here," Elizabeth answered, pushing her hair behind her ear as she picked up the telephone. Halfway through her conversation with the manager of the Reading branch a second light on her telephone lit up and she put the manager on hold while she answered. "Housewares, Miss Chatham speaking."

"Elizabeth, would you believe it, I've found a gown for you—the perfect gown! Do you think you could come home early tonight?"

"Gammy?" Elizabeth questioned blankly, still mentally trying to figure out what the postal service could possibly have done with the cookie cutters. "We've tried every bridal shop in town with no luck. Thank goodness we got that last store to put a rush on the bridesmaids' gowns; at least we have that done. I thought we'd agreed to take the bus into New York City on Friday."

She could hear her grandmother's derisive sniff through the receiver. "There's nothing in New York that could hold a candle to this particular gown," she assured her granddaughter loftily. "Trust me in this, Elizabeth. Have I ever let you down before?"

Out of the corner of her eye Elizabeth could see

the light that showed her the Reading manager was still waiting, and now a third light had begun to blink on the console. "Look, Gammy, I really can't talk about gowns now, much as I'd love to. I have to work until closing tonight and again tomorrow, so I won't be home until after nine either night. Can't this wait until Friday? And you do realize that if this gown isn't right, we'll have lost the day in New York."

"Friday at ten o'clock should be just fine," Rose agreed with unusual docility, then added, "and don't waste time arguing with me. Don't you have a job to do or something? I'm hanging up now."

Pulling the receiver away from her ear, Elizabeth looked at it owlishly for a moment before pressing the button that would reconnect her with the Reading manager. Dealing with the problem in short, if not entirely satisfactory, order, she took the waiting call only to hear her sister Megan whine: "*Gammy* said we can't carry roses because cousin Lisa sneezes. Did you ever hear anything so silly? Liz, you know how I *love* roses. Do we have to listen to Gammy? This is *your* wedding, right?"

"I used to think so," Elizabeth quipped, although she doubted her sister understood her sarcasm. "And I thought you stayed home from school today because you had a headache. Shouldn't you be in bed?''

''*Bed!* Really, Lizzie, how can I stay in bed? I'm telling you, Gammy is going to goof up this whole wedding. She's on the phone all the time with Nick's father, planning everything. Dad's really beginning to get mad. Of course I have a headache. How could I help it?''

''Miss Chatham? Excuse me, but do those spaghetti bowls we got in last week come in any other color except red? My customer says her kitchen is orange, and red will clash.''

Turning toward the open door of her office, Elizabeth looked at Judy and blinked twice as Megan kept up a running list of complaints in her ear, her tale of woe now having something to do with Paul, who said he was going to drink the champagne toast no matter what their father said about substituting ginger ale in his children's glasses. ''What, Judy?'' she asked, feeling a headache of her own coming on. She laid the receiver on the desk and looked through a stack of computer pages that lay to one side.

''Oh, yes, here it is. Blue. They also come in blue, but tell her we'll have to special order it for her,'' she answered before picking up the telephone once more to find that Megan was still talking. ''Meg, I have to go now. We'll talk later, okay?'' she broke in, and then quickly hung up the receiver before her sister could protest.

No sooner was the receiver back in its cradle than the telephone rang again. ''Hello, darling,'' she heard Nick say, and instantly she felt the tension in her shoulder blades beginning to ease.

''Nick! Oh, you don't know how good it is to hear your voice,'' she confessed, clutching the receiver with both hands. ''We're still on for lunch, aren't we? Please, darling, don't fail me now. I think I'm losing my grip on reality.''

''Well, actually, honey, that's why I'm calling,'' Nick began, and Elizabeth's shoulders tensed again. ''Dad just stopped by to talk to me about the wedding, and he wants to join us.''

''Oh, no!'' Elizabeth groaned. ''It's been a madhouse here all morning. I was so looking forward to a few minutes of sanity with you.''

''Is that all I can offer you?'' Nick teased. ''Thanks a lot. You make me sound like a comfortable old shoe, and we've been engaged less than a week.''

''Is that all? I feel like we've been going round and round about this wedding forever. And keep your voice down, darling, or your father will hear you, and I wouldn't want to hurt him for the world. What does he want now? He and Dad aren't fighting over the band again, are they? I thought that was all settled.''

''Bingo, darling—plus one,'' Nick answered, letting her know that she was right, he wasn't alone and yes, trouble was brewing once more.

''It *is* the band—and the reception, too, right?'' she asked, sagging against the back of the chair. ''They seemed to understand each other so well when we went to your father's house for dinner last Saturday. Nick—what do you say we elope? It'd be a lot easier, and then we can be alone. Just think of it!''

''You certainly do pick your times, don't you, darling?'' Nick whispered into the telephone, and Elizabeth knew the idea appealed to him, as well. Then, louder, he went on, ''So we're all set, right, sweetheart? We'll meet you downstairs in the restaurant at one o'clock. What, Dad? Oh, sure, I'll tell her. Elizabeth, Dad says to bring your appetite with you; it's his treat.''

''And if Halloween weren't already past, I'd say it's probably going to be his 'trick,' as well,'' Elizabeth concluded aloud, smiling as she heard Nick's soft baritone chuckle. ''I love you, darling,'' she said and smiled as he told her that he loved her, too.

After hanging up the telephone for what she hoped was the last time for a while, Elizabeth reconsidered her earlier thought. Life was indeed wonderful. However, with every passing day, it was also getting to be more and more complicated.

Judy Holland poked her head in through the open office door again, calling, "Miss Chatham, the lady says blue will clash with the orange, too. Do you have it in yellow? And, oh, I almost forgot. Your mother is here with some swatches for the bridesmaids' gowns you picked out last week; something about your grandmother saying you'll have to find silk flowers to match the color. Something about somebody sneezing, I think she said. She showed them to me and I think the pink would be pretty, but of course it's your choice. Shall I send her back here or do you want to come out on the floor?"

Elizabeth allowed her forehead to fall into her hands as she released her breath in a long, exasperated sigh, wondering if all brides had to ride this same dizzy carousel of happiness and frustration.

Nick picked Elizabeth up at home at nine o'clock the following morning, knowing she wasn't scheduled to start work until noon. He hadn't told her where they were going, and it pleased him to hear her squeal of surprise and delight when he pulled his car into the driveway behind the Tudor house on Prospect Avenue.

"You remembered! Oh, you darling!" Elizabeth cried, catapulting herself across the console to give him a hug. "Is that the realtor? Is the house empty? I haven't seen lights inside it for the past week. I thought you forgot, not that I would have blamed you. Oh, this is going to be such fun. Gammy will be green with envy when I tell her I finally got to see the inside of the 'castle.'"

"The answers are yes, yes, and, if you tell your grandmother about this I will personally wring your neck," Nick answered, helping Elizabeth as she excitedly scrambled out of the car, not willing to waste any time waiting for him to come around and open her car door. "If we're going to play house, as you call it, Elizabeth my love, the last thing we need to do is tell Rose about it, right?"

Instantly Elizabeth was sorry she had mentioned her grandmother's name. For the moment, she felt that both of them had had enough of their relatives. After surviving the trying lunch they'd had with Nick's father the day before, they had been treated to another scene last night on Spring Street that had featured both fathers and Elizabeth's grandmother in the starring roles.

As Megan had said, Rose was now spending time with Henry Lancaster—nearly every day—

and was solidly on that man's side when it came to having the reception at his country club; she had no qualms about stating her arguments to her son. For his part, Elizabeth's father, who had previously agreed to using the country club as long as he could choose the band, had turned stubborn when Henry reacted to Jimmy Timenski and His Polka Dots with barely concealed scorn.

Of course, there was also the very delicate matter of just who was going to pay for everything. The church hall was within Jack Chatham's price range; the country club was not. Rose's offer to share the cost was refused out of hand, and for a while Elizabeth was afraid there was going to be a real family battle, but in the end Nick had settled everything brilliantly.

After excusing himself to confer at some length with his father by telephone, he had announced that the expenses would be split three ways, with the parents taking a share each and he and Elizabeth paying for a third themselves. Furthermore, he had pronounced in his most businesslike way, the reception would have to be held at the country club, but only because the church hall could not hold the number of people that were to be invited.

But the best part of all—the part that still had Elizabeth chuckling every time she thought about it—had been Nick's solution to "the battle of the bands.'' The Great Room at the club, a separate area away from the main dining room that had a floor designed specifically for dancing, was a very large chamber, big enough to accommodate two bandstands. Richard Burrows and his Orchestra would set up their instruments at one end, and Jimmy Timenski and his Polka Dots would be at the other end, accordion and all. When one band was taking a break, the other would play.

"And if you don't like that, you and my father can darn well *hum* the tunes, because that's the best compromise I can work out,'' Nick had concluded so forcefully that not even the outspoken Rose had dared to object.

"Oh, how I love a masterful man!'' Megan had gushed, clasped hands to her breast as she had pretended to swoon onto the couch, breaking the tension and allowing everyone to laugh and shake hands.

Jack and Gloria had quickly admitted their relief to Nick, thanking him for his help as Paul and John went off to watch professional wrestling on television, saying that at least then they could see a *good* fight. Megan had waited until her brothers had left the room to sidle up to Nick and ask his opinion of her new perfume, while Rose had gone back to her endless lists, saying something about adding twenty more people now that she knew the size of the room.

Marrying a successful businessman had its perks, Elizabeth confided to Nick later on the front porch while across the street Mrs. Williamson watched them from behind her lace curtains. "You're fair, but firm. I believe I like that in a man," she teased, kissing his chin. "Mmm, delicious. You smell almost as good as Megan does. I think she's trying out her feminine wiles on you; but she can't have you. I saw you first. Kiss me, you masterful man."

"Don't push me, lady, I don't have much to lose," Nick had returned, running his fingers lightly across her midriff, knowing she was ticklish, loving Elizabeth's squeals as she struggled within his grasp. Mrs. Williamson's lace curtains had immediately opened wide and Nick and Elizabeth ended up holding on to each other, giggling like guilty children.

With the relief they had felt now that the wedding plans were at last settled—at least some of them, that is—they deserved this "playtime" today, as Nick referred to it before they followed the Realtor to the front door.

Once there, Nick deftly removed the key from the Realtor's hand and said politely but firmly, "Thank you very much, Mr. Carlson. We'll drop this off at your office when we're done. Come on, darling.''

Elizabeth, her hand firmly gripped by Nick's, could only smile politely at the bemused salesman as she was tugged along behind Nick into the house, the door closing in Mr. Carlson's face. ''I think that might have been rude, darling,'' she pointed out pleasantly as she looked around the two-story-high foyer. ''He must have rehearsed his sales pitch for hours, poor man.''

''Yes, it was, wasn't it?'' Nick agreed, unrepentant. ''You and Rose were right, Elizabeth. It is a gallery staircase, and the wood carving is beautiful. Where do you want to start, upstairs or down?''

Suddenly Elizabeth missed the realtor. The house was empty, their voices echoing against the high ceiling, and she fought to keep the atmosphere light so that it wouldn't look the way it felt—like she was alone in the house of her dreams with the man of her dreams. After all, they were only playing; only looking. She certainly didn't expect Nick to buy this house for her. It must cost the earth, for one thing, and—oh, who did she think she was kidding? She had only seen the foyer, and already she was falling madly in love with the house.

''Why don't we start down here?'' she decided at last, not ready to go upstairs and see the bedrooms.

It was a large house, as big inside as it appeared from the outside, with a number of high, multi-paned casement windows and three sets of French doors leading out to the patio that wrapped around two sides of the house. And yet, Elizabeth decided as they stood in the living room and looked through to the library, it was a cozy house. It had lots of corners and hidden nooks and crannies to make it feel homey. She especially liked the wide window seat set in one corner of the dining room, its view looking out over the back garden and a large, droopy willow tree. It was a place made for dreaming.

"What did you think of the kitchen, darling?" Nick asked as they walked back into the foyer. "It certainly seems to have everything in it."

"And then some," Elizabeth agreed, remembering the wide center island that contained the six-burner stove complete with indoor grill. "My mother would love it, as she's the gourmet cook in our household. But don't worry, she taught me well, I promise you. Why, I can even bake my own bread."

"And I can whip up anything that comes in its own disposable tray and fits into a microwave," he replied, dropping a quick kiss on the top of her head. "At least we won't starve." Wrapping an arm around her waist, Nick led the way up the wide, curved staircase, preferring to see the upstairs for the first time this way rather than by using the narrower set of steps they had discovered in the service hallway behind the kitchen.

The wide upper landing wrapped around the front of the house, with three oversize windows admitting a warming stream of early morning sunlight, while a high carved railing kept the center open to the foyer below. There was a large square hallway behind that opening, with doors leading off in every direction.

They discovered five bedrooms and three bathrooms. The smallest bedroom also had a wide window seat, and Elizabeth could easily imagine the room as a nursery, with white organdy tieback curtains on the windows and a large rocking chair in the corner.

But it was the master bedroom that seemed to hold Nick's interest. More than just a room with connecting bath, it was a suite with two dressing rooms and a pair of walk-in closets on either side of one of the large dormer windows. Even his king-size bed would be swallowed up in the massive room.

"So, all done playing, sweetheart?" he asked, leading her from the room and back toward the stairs. "It's getting late, and we still have to take the key back to the Realtor. Are you ready?"

Still looking over her shoulder, Elizabeth followed meekly until they were back in the downstairs foyer once more. It was over. He had said they would look at the house and they had looked at the house. It was fun, granted, but she knew that was all it had been. They had already decided that they would live in Nick's apartment after the wedding, at least until they had time to catch their breath and make plans to settle themselves permanently.

After all, she had just begun her job. Although Nick had offered to let her resign in order to concentrate on the wedding, Elizabeth had decided to stay on, knowing how difficult it would be to replace her on such short notice in the middle of the busy Christmas season.

But, rational reasoning to one side, Elizabeth had fallen deeply in love with this house. It had always intrigued her, sparked her imagination; but now that she had walked through it, heard the voices of her yet-to-be-born children laughing in the halls, and seen a misty picture of Nick and herself readying themselves for bed in their private suite as the light from the fireplace danced warm and golden across the pitched stucco ceiling, she knew this was a house she could never forget.

It was silly. She was being impractical. She was also being greedy. She had Nick; she already had everything she could ever want. A house was just a house, nothing more. "I'm ready," she said at last, giving the place one last look. "Playtime's over, alas, and it's back to the real world. I have some Christmas tree cookie cutters to locate before the day is out."

Nick locked the front door and turned toward her questioningly. "You want to run that one by me one more time? We just got done looking at one terrific house, and all you can talk about are some cookie cutters? I think you have some explaining to do."

Elizabeth reached up on tiptoe and kissed his cheek. "No, I don't. I am about to be a bride. I'm allowed to be vague. In fact, I'm beginning to think 'vague' is a required course for brides. That and Harassed 101. But please let me thank you, darling. I just loved seeing the house."

"Did it live up to your expectations?" Nick held open the car door as he waited for her answer.

"Well, the faucets in the bathroom weren't solid gold, but then one can't have everything, now can one?" she tossed back at him, busily arranging her skirt on the leather seat while she averted her eyes. "Silly man! Of course it lived up to my expectations. A person would have to be crazy not to love that place."

Nick closed the door and took his time walking

around the car to get in on the driver's side. Sliding in behind the steering wheel, his expression kind, he said, "Maybe in a few years, when we're seriously looking for a place of our own, we'll consider building a Tudor."

Elizabeth commanded her facial muscles to form a smile. "What a wonderful idea, darling. In a few years, when we're ready. This house is lovely, but it's really much too big for two people, isn't it?"

Nick shrugged. "Well, I don't know. We could always set up a bowling alley in the foyer," he said facetiously, earning himself a jab in the ribs from Elizabeth's elbow before he changed the subject to a problem he was having with the new computers in the credit office, and the discussion of the Tudor house on Prospect Avenue was dropped once and for all.

Chapter Seven

"I didn't know there were any bridal shops out this way, Gammy." Elizabeth was beginning to wonder just where her grandmother's directions were taking them. The woman had been behaving strangely ever since she had first mentioned the "dream gown" and now that they were at last on their way to the store, Elizabeth couldn't help thinking that the woman looked ready to burst with excitement. "Are you sure we're going the right way? I could be home addressing invitations."

"Just hush up and turn right at the next corner, Elizabeth." Rose squirmed in the passenger seat of her son's station wagon and patted the large rectangular box perched across her knees. "What do you think I'm doing, kidnapping you?"

"I don't know, do I?" Elizabeth answered, taking her gaze from the road for a moment to look inquisitively at the box. "For all I know, you could have a submachine gun stashed in that thing. Why won't you tell me what you've got in there?"

Rose looked at her granddaughter with an expression that reminded Elizabeth of the Cheshire cat in *Alice's Adventures in Wonderland* and said, "In good time, darling, all in good time. Here's the turn."

Putting on the turn signal automatically, Elizabeth had the station wagon well into the turn before she realized that they were now on Macada Drive. "There's nothing out this way but houses, Gammy. As a matter of fact, Nick's father lives just one more block down this road. But you know that, don't you? Gammy—"

"Pull in Henry's driveway, Elizabeth, and park the car," Rose ordered, adding, "and for pity's sake, close your mouth. Henry's standing at the door, waiting for us."

Rose was right; Henry Lancaster was standing just inside the open door, the smile on his face doing strange things to Elizabeth's insides. "What have you two hatched between you this time, Gammy?" she asked, beginning to worry. "I know the two of you have had your heads together on everything from the menu for the reception to the flowers we're carrying, but don't you think I'm even capable of finding my own wedding gown?''

Sliding out of the passenger seat still balancing the large box, Rose tut-tutted her granddaughter's outburst and practically skipped up the shallow stairs to say hello to her old friend. ''I tell you, it was like pulling teeth, Hank, but I got her here. Is everything ready?''

''Of course,'' Henry informed her with a wink. ''Good morning, Elizabeth. You look lovely today. Your mother's here, waiting for you. We've had a nice chat about your school days. You didn't tell me you played the piccolo in the marching band. Would you like Mrs. Gillespie to serve coffee or do you want to see the gown right away?''

Once inside the house Elizabeth saw that her mother was indeed there, holding a cup of coffee as she stood in the entrance to the living room. ''Mom? I don't understand. What are you doing here?''

''I came to see you in the gown, of course,'' Gloria Chatham answered matter-of-factly. ''Henry and your grandmother were kind enough to have included me in the surprise. After all, I am the mother of the bride, aren't I? It's lovely, by the way. Henry let me see it.''

''I don't believe this; I don't believe any of this.'' Elizabeth didn't know whether to laugh or cry. Obviously she and her mother had been brought here on a wild-goose chase to play unwilling parts in her grandmother's latest flight of fancy. She loved Gammy, she really did, and she wouldn't want to insult Nick's father, but enough was enough. Nobody—but *nobody*—was going to choose her wedding gown for her!

Opening her mouth to say just that, Elizabeth was astounded to hear herself meekly agreeing to follow Mrs. Gillespie upstairs to try on the gown.

"Here, darling, take this with you," Rose called after her as Elizabeth mounted the first step. "There's a full slip in it and the headpiece you liked at that shop in Allentown last week. Just to help you judge the gown with all the right accessories, of course," she added lamely as Elizabeth looked daggers at her. "Now, shoo! Hank and Gloria and I will wait down here for your entrance."

"Do you believe those two, Mrs. Gillespie?" Elizabeth questioned in exasperation as the housekeeper opened the door to one of the bedrooms. "Gammy even roped my mother in this time. You know, my grandmother picked out my gown for my senior prom, now that I think of it, and even called my date to instruct him on what sort of flowers he was to bring. I love Gammy, honestly I do, but this time I think she's gone too—*oh, look at that!*"

"Beautiful, isn't it?" Mrs. Gillespie walked across the room to where a wedding gown was hanging from an open closet door, its long train tumbled onto the carpet. "It was Mrs. Lancaster's," she explained as she reverently touched the skirt, lightly fluffing it. "They just don't make things like this anymore. Do you know, every single pearl and sequin on this entire gown was sewn on individually? She had it preserved, thank goodness, and Mr. Lancaster had it taken out and pressed for you to see it. I think he's right, it should be almost a perfect fit. You do want to try it on, don't you?"

Elizabeth couldn't speak, but only raised her hands toward the gown a few times as she walked across the room, before stopping in front of it, her bottom lip quivering. Her eyes filled with tears as she stood, transfixed, staring at the most beautiful gown she'd ever seen. "It—it's lovely—gorgeous. Truly. I—"

Mrs. Gillespie, seeing that Elizabeth was on the verge of breaking down, became all business. Going over to the bed and the box that she had laid on the bedspread, she lifted the lid and pulled out the slip, corselette and headpiece she knew she would find there. After draping them across the bed she walked up behind Elizabeth and helped the stunned girl remove her suit jacket. "That's a good girl. Now, what do you say we give them a show?''

Fifteen minutes later Mrs. Gillespie walked down the wide mahogany staircase and summoned Henry, Gloria and Rose into the foyer. They stood on the black-and-white tiles beneath the crystal chandelier and craned their heads upward for their first sight of Elizabeth.

She walked slowly out onto the wide upstairs landing, trying hard to decide if she felt more like Cinderella at the ball or Scarlett O'Hara on her way to a party. She felt beautiful, yet fragile, and more completely feminine than at any other time of her life.

The full ballroom skirt of heavy *peau de soie* billowed over the half-dozen underslips that rustled faintly with her every step, and the pearls and scattering of sequins decorating the floral-design reembroidered alençon lace that accented the bodice and swirled across the skirt sparkled as they caught the light.

The gown had a Basque waist that outlined her slim form perfectly, and her shoulders rose creamily above the off-the-shoulder neckline; the short puffed sleeves standing out to each side just enough to give balance to the full skirt. Age had lent a peachy-beige tone to the gown; the material had a richness and depth to it that Elizabeth had not seen in any of the gowns she'd looked at, and dismissed, in the bridal shops.

The headpiece that Rose had included was the delicate alençon-lace and pearl crown Elizabeth had chosen at one of the shops, with the layer upon layer of tulle attached to the back of the crown adding a heightened pouf while allowing enough veiling for a modest fingertip veil.

She knew how she looked, for Mrs. Gillespie had placed her in front of a full-length mirror before leaving the room, but the expression on her mother's face reinforced her feeling of ethereal beauty.

As she approached the stairway and began her descent, the cathedral-length train swept along behind her. The large flat *peau de soie* bow near the bottom edge of the train matched the bows floating on either side of the skirt below her hips. With her hands lifting the full skirt just slightly above her ankles, her eyelids now lowered to avoid contact with anyone else, she felt herself float down the staircase, a fairy princess, an angel—a bride!

"Just the way my Katherine looked on our wedding day." Henry's voice was choked with emotion, and he reached into his pocket to take out a handkerchief and unashamedly dab at his eyes.

"Oh, Elizabeth!" Gloria gushed, bursting into tears. "You're so lovely!"

Rose was also crying, but she was smiling through her tears, knowing that this moment was so perfect, so healing, so absolutely right. "My granddaughter's quite a girl, isn't she, Hank?"

Elizabeth walked up to Henry and kissed him on the cheek. "I—I don't know how to thank you, Mr. Lancaster. This—well, this is just the most beautiful gown in the world. I'm more than flattered—I'm *honored* that you'd allow me to wear it."

Henry returned her kiss, then said, "You just make my son happy, all right? And give me a few grandchildren before I get much older."

Her face losing its solemn beauty to beam brightly as she smiled, Elizabeth, tears of happiness standing on her eyelashes, threw her arms around the man and hugged him tightly. "That's a promise, Mr. Lancaster!"

"Dad. That's a promise, Dad," he said gruffly, holding her at arm's length in front of him.

"That's a promise, Dad," Elizabeth repeated as Rose and Mrs. Gillespie hugged each other and congratulated themselves on a job well done.

To bring them all back to earth, Rose announced prosaically: "This is all well and good, but I still say we're having green beans with the filet mignon."

Elizabeth laughed and shook her head. "Back to

that, are we? Gammy, I talked to Nick, and neither he nor I like green beans. We'd rather serve broccoli.''

"Here we go again," Gloria said, sighing resignedly. "Please leave me out of this discussion."

"Thanks, Mom," Elizabeth teased, "I knew I could count on you."

"We're serving green beans," Rose reiterated staunchly, looking to Henry for support. "Everybody else likes them. Besides, you and Nick probably won't remember a thing you eat anyway."

Throwing her arms up in mock surrender, Elizabeth said, "I give up! I'm too happy right now to fight with you. Green beans it is. Mom, Mrs. Gillespie, would you please help me with the gown? I don't want to soil it."

As Elizabeth disappeared back up the stairs with her mother, the housekeeper holding her train for her as she went, Rose nudged Henry in the ribs with her elbow. "See what I mean, Hank? It's all in the timing. We'll get those trumpets in the choir loft yet, I promise. Now, why don't we go over that seating chart again while we're waiting for Gloria and Elizabeth? You did say you wanted the mayor at the same table as the senator?''

"Good Lord, no!" Henry replied, following

Rose into the living room. "They can't stand each other. Let me get the chart and we'll go over it again."

Thanksgiving came and Gloria invited Henry and Nick to dinner, which was an enormous meal that always took her days to prepare, just so that her family could wolf it all down during halftime of one of the many football games that kept the men hidden in the den for most of the day.

This year, however, she warned her family that things would be different. After sampling what dinner was like at Henry's house, with Mrs. Gillespie serving course after course in the elegant dining room, Gloria had worked herself into a frenzy, polishing every bit of silver and hand washing her good china and crystal.

Rose did her part by obligingly unearthing a handmade lace tablecloth her own mother had brought over from Ireland a lifetime earlier and Elizabeth and Megan had set the table after Paul and John inserted the extra leaf.

By noon everything was ready and the appetite-inducing smell of roasting turkey filled the house, along with the pleasing but not so traditional aroma of spaghetti sauce and meatballs bubbling on top of the stove. Elizabeth didn't question the spaghetti, as it had been served on every holiday in her memory, right alongside the cranberry sauce and half a dozen assorted vegetables. It was a family favorite, and a family tradition.

It was, however, a revelation to Nick and Henry, but Gloria's excellent cooking overshadowed their surprise and soon they were all seated around the large dining-room table, passing plates and talking about the quarterbacks for the next game, due on at six o'clock.

"I'm telling you, Megan could throw better than that guy," Paul said as he reached in front of Henry for the mashed potatoes, just to have his grandmother deftly smack the back of his hand with a tablespoon. "Ouch! Hey, Gammy, cut that out!"

"Got you that time," John crowed, laughing. "Remember what Mom told us; no boardinghouse reach today."

If Gloria had worried that Henry Lancaster would feel overwhelmed by her noisy, boisterous family she soon relaxed as Henry said, "Paul, I can remember my mother doing the same thing to me that your grandmother just did to you when there was company for dinner. But Nick and I aren't company; we're family. Isn't that right, Jack?"

Jack Chatham, standing at the end of the table as he carved the turkey, replied, "We certainly are,

Henry. Would you like white meat or dark? I'm afraid Megan already has dibs on one of the legs."

"Oh, Father, please," Megan complained in a pained voice, eyeing Nick to see if he had noticed her new sweater. "Let the boys have the legs. They're too messy."

"Well, la-di-da," John said singsong. "Would you listen to her? *Father*. Hah!"

Nick reached for and found Elizabeth's hand under the table. "One more month," he whispered, "and we'll be having dinner in our own place."

"Yes," Elizabeth agreed on a sigh. "Alone. Won't it be heaven?"

"Nick!" his father commanded, interrupting his son just as he was leaning toward Elizabeth's mouth. "Stop eating that poor child with your eyes and pass me some more of those meatballs. Gloria, this is delicious. I can't remember the last time I tasted anything this good. You'll have to give Mrs. Gillespie your recipe."

The meal was a success; Gloria's pumpkin pie was its usual triumph, and Nick and Elizabeth were told to go amuse themselves somehow while the women cleaned up the kitchen and the men returned to the den for the football game. They didn't have to be asked twice, quickly taking up their coats and heading for the backyard.

Once outside on the porch in the deepening

dusk, Nick quickly pulled Elizabeth into his arms and soundly kissed her. "God, but I needed that!" he breathed against her ear. "Out of town all week opening that branch in Delaware and then seeing you for the first time surrounded by our families. Tell me, when was the last time we were alone? I mean *really* alone?"

Elizabeth moved her head slightly to one side so that he could nuzzle the base of her throat with his lips. "Do those five minutes in your office Monday morning before you left for Delaware mean anything?"

Nick's response was a low growl.

"No, I didn't think so," she answered, running a hand into the hair at the back of his neck. "You want to go to a movie?"

Nick stood slightly away from her and arched his eyebrows at her, replying, "Only if you promise we can neck in the back of the balcony."

"Nicholas Lancaster," Elizabeth declared, pretending to pout, "there are times I believe you only want me for my body."

"Really? And does that bother you?"

Elizabeth grinned. "Nope, seeing that I kinda like your body, too."

"That does it! Let's get out of here," Nick decided, pulling her toward the back door. "We'll tell them we're going to the movies and then—"

"And then—what?" Elizabeth asked, trying not to mention their pact of purposely staying away from closed, intimate places.

Nick, who had visions of his apartment dancing in his head, came back to reality with a depressing bang. Shrugging, he looked around, trying to form an idea. When his gaze locked on the Christmas Star shining on South Mountain he said abruptly: "We're going to take a ride and look at the Christmas lights. Nothing can be any more harmless than that."

Within five minutes they were on their way out the front door, Nick carrying a large plastic container filled with sliced turkey and stuffing that Gloria had insisted he take home with him. After he stashed the container on the floor behind the driver's seat and started the engine, Elizabeth suggested they should start their tour by riding across the Hill to Hill Bridge two blocks away.

"Do you remember how the bridge used to look when they put a tree in the circle in the middle of the intersection?" Elizabeth asked as they drove along. "The traffic jams were horrendous, with people and tour buses coming from all over to see the tree, but it certainly was beautiful. Sometimes progress can be a little sad. When I was a Girl Scout, we'd all hike across the bridge, singing carols as we went."

"You must have made a great Girl Scout," Nick commented, still intent on finding some place to be alone with her. "I would have bought all your cookies."

"Oh, Nick, look," Elizabeth exclaimed, purposely ignoring his remark. "Moravian College has candles in all the windows of the buildings. I love those old stone dormitories. You know, the early Moravians were very big on Christmas. The crèche at the Moravian Church is absolutely beautiful. Let's drive by it, all right?"

Nick knew when he was beaten, and secretly he also knew that Elizabeth was right. They were going to do this thing right. They had already been through their required meeting with the priest, and they were planning a serious ceremony. He was a grown man; he wasn't some hot-blooded young boy who could put his own pleasure ahead of everything else and damn the consequences.

But that didn't mean it was easy; he loved Elizabeth so much, wanted her so much. And she felt the same way, which was the other reason he knew he could wait for their wedding night before making her completely his. Their love was special, and the celebration of that love had to be just as special. Yet it was only Thanksgiving. How would he ever wait until the day after Christmas?

Elizabeth reached across the seat to take hold of

Nick's hand, sensing the tension in his body and knowing what he was thinking. "I love you so much," she said softly. "You make me feel so cherished, darling, so special. If we could, I'd love to run away tonight and get married. But I want to come to you the way your mother came to your father, even wearing the gown she wore. It's silly, I guess, and if anyone had asked me a year ago if I would feel this way I would have said they were crazy, but—"

"But love does strange things to people," Nick ended for her. "And it is crazy. Here I am, Nicholas Lancaster, owner of a fair-size department store chain, reduced to driving around town stealing kisses at stop lights. You know, if it had been up to us, we would have been married by now. We aren't children; we don't need all this ceremony. How did we let ourselves get talked into this?"

It was worse than Elizabeth had feared. Nick was really beginning to hate the delay, to hate the whole idea of a big wedding. Unfortunately as each day passed, and certainly ever since trying on Katherine Lancaster's gown, Elizabeth was getting more and more caught up in the idea of a lavish wedding.

Yet, she reasoned silently, when she really came down to thinking about it, becoming Mrs. Nicholas Lancaster was what she really wanted. Maybe the strain was too much for them; if she wasn't careful they would soon be arguing, and all because of a silly wedding.

"You want to go to Maryland for breakfast, Nick?" she asked at last, watching his face as they passed beneath a street lamp glittering with Christmas lights.

Nick darted a questioning look at her as he turned the car onto a side road at the base of South Mountain. "Maryland? Breakfast? Has that wine Dad brought to dinner gone to your head?"

"I think so," Elizabeth answered slowly, "because I'm offering to elope with you—tonight. We can drive down to Maryland, find a justice of the peace and stick around for breakfast before we drive back."

"Just in time to break the news to your family and my father. Are you harboring a death wish you haven't told me about, darling?"

The idea of eloping appealed to Nick, it appealed to him more than he'd ever admit to Elizabeth, but he couldn't ask her to sacrifice her dreams just because he couldn't seem to control his passion to take her to his bed. "Besides, think of Jimmy Timenski and His Polka Dots. Your father tells me they've been practicing every night at the Legion Hall down the street. What could we say to them?"

Elizabeth put a hand over her mouth to stifle a giggle. "And think of all those green beans going to waste," she added, her relief making her feel slightly giddy. "It's almost criminal. Where are we?"

Nick pulled the car off to the side of the narrow gravel road and turned off the key. "All that talk about your exploits as a Girl Scout brought back memories of my Boy Scout days. Every Christmas we'd climb up here to sing Christmas carols beneath the star. So many different groups did the same thing that it used to get pretty crowded up here every night. See," he said, pointing toward the front windshield, "there's the star, straight ahead."

Nick helped her out of the car and they approached the massive scaffolding that supported the five-pointed star. "It must be forty or fifty feet high," Elizabeth remarked, craning her neck to see to the top of the highest point.

"Fifty-three feet," Nick told her, "if I remember it right, although I can't remember how many lights are on it; hundreds and hundreds. Impressive isn't it?"

"Well, Bethlehem is supposed to be the Christmas City," Elizabeth pointed out, proud of her hometown. "It's only fitting that we have a proper Christmas star. People can see it for miles."

Nick looked at Elizabeth's face, glowing from the reflected light high above them, thinking she had never looked more beautiful. Her cherry-red cape was appropriate for this, the official launching of the Christmas season and for once he was not dreading the hectic days that stretched between now and the close of business Christmas Eve. He only hoped he could be kept so busy that the time would pass swiftly.

"Oh Nick, darling, look," Elizabeth cried excitedly, holding out her hands. "It's beginning to snow. The flakes are huge!"

The snow floated down slowly, catching in Elizabeth's auburn hair and dusting the shoulders of her cape as she spun around in a circle; her arms were outstretched like a small child trying to catch the snow.

Nick knew he was lost. As Elizabeth stopped her whirling, her cheeks flushed from the cold air, a smile lighting her face, he drew her gently into his arms and lowered his face to hers. "I love you, Elizabeth Chatham," he vowed huskily. "I love you so very, very much."

The world faded away as they clung to each other beneath the Christmas star, the snow increasing in intensity so that it swirled around them, dusting the gravel path and clinging to the bare branches of the low trees that crowded the hillside.

His mouth slanted first this way, then that against hers as she opened to him, allowing herself to be drawn more deeply into the kiss. With one hand at the back of her head, he held her against him, tasting her sweetness, as his other hand crept inside the cherry-red cape to caress her small waist. ''I love you, Elizabeth,'' he breathed into her mouth, ''I love you, I love you, I love you.''

Straining against him, desperate to be closer to him, Elizabeth lost all sense of time and place, of right and wrong, wanting only to please him, to be pleased by him. There was more to love than hearts and flowers, and this deep need to physically belong to each other couldn't be ignored any longer. She was his, she wanted to be his in every way.

''Hey, guys, look at that! There's a couple of people over here—necking!''

Nick pulled back at the sound of a young boy calling to his friends, to see a troop of Boy Scouts coming up the roadway, their scoutmaster huffing and puffing as he brought up the rear. Bringing himself back under control with some difficulty, Nick quipped, ''Some traditions die hard in Bethlehem, don't they, darling? It would seem the Boy Scout pilgrimage to the star is one of them.''

Hiding her face against his jacket, Elizabeth could only nod her head, not trusting her voice until they had walked past the scout troop and reached the car. "Nick," she said as he helped her into the passenger side of the car, "do you ever get the feeling Gammy has put a hex on us?"

"What do you mean?"

"I mean, we can't seem to be alone even when we're on the side of a mountain. Now tell me, doesn't that seem a little farfetched to be simple coincidence—or even pure bad luck?"

Nick started the engine, then turned the car back down the hill the way they had come. "I refuse to answer on the grounds it may scare the hell out of me. Oh well, darling, I think I can have you back home in time for the second half of the football game. John said he'd save me a seat on the end of the couch."

"Well yippee, and bully for you," Elizabeth groused, sinking down in her seat. "Sure, you can go hide in the den. I bet we won't be back in the house five minutes before they all start on me again because we haven't auditioned a soloist yet for the church. And tomorrow's Black Friday, the busiest shopping day of the year. My life is just one unending stream of fun, fun, fun these days. I don't know how I handle the sheer excitement of it."

"Poor baby," he commiserated with exaggerated concern.

Raising her hands threateningly, Elizabeth

warned tightly, "Don't push your luck, buster. These hands are registered with the police."

"But you love me," Nick reminded her happily, amazed at the way they could go from heated passion to silly teasing so quickly, so easily.

"But I love you," she agreed, moving as close as the console allowed to sit with her head resting against his shoulder. "Nick," she asked idly as they drove back across town to Spring Street, "do you think Prince Andrew and his Fergie had all these problems?"

Chapter Eight

"That's funny," Nick remarked as they pulled up in front of the Chatham house, "Dad's car is still here. I would have thought he'd be long gone by now. I think I'd better go inside with you, darling."

Elizabeth looked at him warily, not liking the apprehension she heard in his voice. "You don't think someone's ill, do you?"

Putting a hand under her elbow as they mounted the porch steps, Nick said, "No, darling, not ill. If this prickling at the back of my neck means anything, I have a feeling we're in for another discussion about the wedding. But besides the prickle, I guess I should tell you, I've been hiding something from you, hoping Dad would change his mind."

Elizabeth felt her stomach drop to her toes. "What is it? Don't tell me we're back to the battle of the bands. You seemed to have settled that so well."

"If only it was that easy. No, it's not about the bands." Nick stopped on the porch and drew her to one side. "I have a confession to make to you about my father, darling. Brace yourself—it isn't pretty."

Elizabeth's cheeks paled. "He hates me," she breathed, grabbing Nick's arm. "Oh, I just knew things were going too well. Everyone I talk to says there are all sorts of problems with families before a wedding. My friend Beth told me about a girl who works with her, and she had the most awful time trying to—"

Nick kissed Elizabeth to cut off the flow of words, then said, "Dad doesn't hate you, darling. As a matter of fact, there have been times these past few weeks when I've thought he's merely tolerating me because it's through me that he's discovered you and rediscovered Rose."

Now Elizabeth was angry. What was Nick trying to do—frighten her into cardiac arrest? "Well, then, what is it? I feel like a thief standing out here, casing the joint or something while I can hear voices inside."

Nick took a deep breath, exhaled it slowly and

said, "My father is a toy junkie. There, it's out in the open."

"A *toy* junkie?" Elizabeth looked at Nick as if to see if he was completely sober. "Oh, well, that's it then—of course you realize, Nicholas, that the wedding's off. I could never be related to a toy junkie. Nick, *what the devil are you talking about?*"

"*Shhh!* They'll hear us," he warned, pulling Elizabeth farther into the shadows. "And stop laughing, dammit, this isn't funny. Look—Dad has always been crazy about toys. Why do you think Lancaster's has all those wild, oversize mechanical monstrosities perched on every floor during the Christmas Season? The man's crazy for toys. Only now, thanks to modern technology, he's found a whole new outlet for his addiction. *Home computers.*"

Elizabeth was still chuckling, although she was trying hard to get a grip on herself, aware that Nick was being deadly serious. "Computers, huh? I can see your problem, darling, as you hate the things."

"A necessary evil," Nick agreed, nodding his head solemnly.

"All right. You've confessed, and now I know all about your father's failings. But I also *fail* to see the connection; I don't understand what all the fuss is about. What can your father's love of home computers possibly have to do with our wedding?''

Nick arched his eyebrows as he pulled her over to the window that looked in on the living room. Just as he had thought, his father and the entire Chatham family were gathered around the coffee table, looking at a portable computer that sat there, it's green eye glowing malevolently, like an alien space creature. ''Do you see that?'' he asked Elizabeth. ''Dad must have brought it with him, the sneak. Some genius has invented a plan-your-wedding program for home computers.''

''Oh, no,'' Elizabeth wailed, rejecting the idea that something as romantic as her wedding day could be turned into a cut-and-dried computer program. ''What are they looking at now?''

Nick bent down to peer through the glass. ''Unless I miss my guess, they're working out the seating chart for the reception.''

''But that's the thing Beth told me her friend and her fiancé nearly broke up over! Oh, Lordy, Nick, we'd better get in there—fast!''

No sooner had they opened the front door than Rose's voice reached them, saying impatiently, ''That's entirely out of the question, Jack. Why would I want to sit next to Margaret? She's *old*— we have nothing in common. I'm not going to spend the whole reception listening to her telling me about her gallbladder operation again. I wonder if she still carries the stones around with her in that little brown bottle? Daft woman.''

"She squeezes my cheeks, Gammy," Megan added, as if to prove her grandmother's point.

"But, Mom," her son protested, "Aunt Margaret is Elizabeth's godmother. She has to sit at the table with us; it says so in the book Gloria found in Elizabeth's room. See—parents may have their own table…sitting with *close relatives*—"

"Close relatives *and friends*," Rose finished for him firmly, looking over his shoulder. "I'm going to sit beside Hank."

"Oh, dear," Gloria asked quietly, "have you forgotten that the groom's family has their own table? Remember, we decided that the families are too large to put them both at the same table."

"Hi, gang," Nick broke in swiftly, realizing that no one had noticed their entrance, "we're back. What's going on? Is Dad teaching the boys how to play football on his computer? I thought the game was still on television."

"Lizzie, you're back!" John exclaimed unnecessarily, scrambling to his feet. "Mom says you're having a bridal table and Megan says that means I can't sit with Eddie and the rest of the guys."

"And we have to be on our best behavior, and Gammy says we have to make sure not to eat like

we're at a trough—just like we were pigs or something, for pete's sake—and then we have to dance
with our partners,'' Paul chimed in, joining his
older brother in their list of complaints. ''You
never said this was going to be such a pain. Me
and John talked about it a couple of minutes ago,
and we decided that we don't want to be in the
wedding anymore, Liz. Sorry about that.''

''John and I,'' Gloria corrected, unruffled.

Helping Elizabeth out of her coat, Nick said
calmly, ''Gee, that's too bad, boys. We'll miss
you, but I guess it can't be helped. Right, darling?''

John frowned, looking at Nick. ''Hey, not so
fast! That's it? We're out of the wedding? But
what about Liz's friends, Nora and Lorraine—
we're supposed to be their partners, aren't we?
You're just gonna let us sit on the sidelines, with
nothing to do? Lizzie?''

Taking her cue from Nick, Elizabeth merely
shrugged, spreading her hands fatalistically.
''What else can we do, boys? I know it's my wedding day, the single most important day of my life,
and it will hurt me deeply if my own brothers don't
want to be a part of it, but I don't want to force
you into anything. If you really want out, you're
out. And no hard feelings, honestly. I'm sure Nick
will have no trouble replacing you.''

"You could use your cousin Steve, Elizabeth," Rose suggested, "and even the boys' friend Eddie, if we're pinched for an extra usher."

Paul glared at his brother angrily. "This is all your fault, you dope. You talked me into this. I *want* to be in the wedding. We told everybody we were going to be wearing tuxes and riding in limousines—and now you've blown the whole thing!"

Nick leaned over and quoted quietly into Elizabeth's ear: "And that's another fine mess you've gotten us into, Stanley." Louder, he said, "Just a minute, Paul—before you get too upset—nothing's written in stone here. If you want back in, just say so. You too, John."

"Only if you agree to play by the rules," Elizabeth added carefully, knowing her brothers much better than Nick did. "And no more plans to wrap Nick's car in plastic wrap so that we can't leave for our honeymoon."

"You overheard us, huh?" John guessed, grimacing. "Eddie said they did it to his cousin's car and it took them over an hour to unwrap it. Okay, we promise to be good, honest."

"Yeah," Paul seconded, then both boys walked over to shake Nick's hand, gratifying their mother who was about to prompt them to do just that from her seat on the ottoman beside the coffee table.

"Can we go watch the end of the football game now, Dad?"

"With my blessing," Jack told them, once more examining the seating chart still dully throbbing on the green computer screen. "I don't know why you even came in here in the first place."

Paul was naive enough to answer: "Because we heard you yelling at Megan and wanted to watch the fun," which earned them a speaking look from their mother and had them bounding out of the room on the double.

"Thank heavens they're gone," Megan pronounced from her tucked-up position in a corner of the slip-covered couch. "See, Mother, I told you the plans should be left to the grown-ups."

"Which of course explains your presence," her grandmother quipped, ruffling Megan's curls and receiving a glare from the youngest Chatham daughter.

Elizabeth walked over to the coffee table and sat down on the floor at Henry Lancaster's feet. "Oh, look, Nick. The whole screen's filled with pictures of round tables, just like at the club. And there's the bridal table—my goodness, it's long, isn't it?"

"It has to hold a bridal party of sixteen, my dear," Henry pointed out, moving the cursor along the sixteen small squares that denoted chairs. "I checked with the manager at the club and she says the table will have to go in front of the windows overlooking the terrace. It's the only place it will fit.''

Nick leaned over his father's shoulder to see the screen. ''I don't like it, Dad. We'll look like the judges' table at an ice-skating competition. I can see it now, Elizabeth—we'll be holding up cards, giving scores on the waitresses for their technical and artistic skill in weaving through the other tables.''

''But it's traditional,'' Rose said, the matter already settled in her own mind.

Elizabeth narrowed her eyes as she looked at the screen. ''You're right, Nick. Besides, so many of the attendants will have wives, husbands or dates with them—like Beth's date from New York—and those people won't know anybody else. I thought we'd dispense with the traditional bridal table and scatter the attendants throughout the room.''

Gloria seemed to like this idea. ''With their pretty plum-colored gowns, the girls would add color to the room, wouldn't they? But, dear, where would you and Nick sit if there isn't going to be a bridal table?''

''With you, of course,'' Elizabeth answered. ''We'll sit with both families, and the priest will also sit at our table. It's quite acceptable, according to the books I've read.''

"And that fool, Margaret?" Rose interposed. "Where does she sit?"

Elizabeth looked to Nick for assistance, and he answered, "I've got an uncle who's ninety and nearly stone-deaf. Aunt Margaret can talk all day long and Uncle Fred will just sit there, nodding and smiling. I think they'd be great together."

The laughter that Nick's solution caused broke some of the tension, but only long enough for Henry to clear the computer screen and begin arranging tables the way Elizabeth had suggested. The long bridal table was discarded in favor of a large circular table placed directly in front of the windows in the middle of the room, and Henry began placing smaller round tables around the room, labeling each with a different letter of the alphabet. "There, now we can seat the rest of the crowd. Elizabeth, where do you want to start?"

The first few tables were filled easily and without any problems, the wedding party being seated with guests close to their own ages. Because of Gloria's suggestion, the bridesmaids were scattered evenly throughout the room, like colorful garnishes tastefully arranged on a platter, and the groomsmen were seated near the dance floor, and away from the bar.

Elizabeth gratefully accepted the glass of white wine Nick handed her, winking at him to show that his fears had been for nothing, just as Henry declared: "Jack, you don't seem to understand. I'm not being a snob. We just can't have Senator Billings sitting at the same table with your friend Harvey."

"Why not?" Jack asked. "Billings is always saying he's plain folks, just like his constituents. Well, Harvey Wycheck is one of his constituents."

"Father," Megan pointed out condescendingly, "Mr. Wycheck is a *garbageman.*"

"Harvey's a businessman. He owns a fleet of waste-disposal trucks. Besides, where would we all be today, I ask you, young lady, if there were no garbagemen?" her father countered.

Rose was happy to enlighten her youngest granddaughter. "Up to our ears in—"

"Mother, please, don't encourage him!" Gloria interrupted before her mother-in-law could say what was on her mind. "Megan, Mr. Wycheck is a lovely man, and captain of your father's bowling team. I suggest you apologize to your father at once and then go out to the kitchen and unload the dishwasher."

"Yes, Mommy," Megan agreed sullenly, pushing herself slowly to her feet. "But I still say Mr. Lancaster is right. Brother, where are you going to put the Mayor—on the other side of Aunt Margaret?"

It was quiet in the room for a few minutes, Henry busily retitling the dozens of little squares and pushing them first to one table, then another, as the sounds of Megan's heavy-handed treatment of her mother's pots and pans filtered into the room.

Finally Henry sat back, sighed and announced proudly. "There, all done. I put the Senator and Mr. Wycheck at the same table and they can talk to each other or ignore each other; it's all the same to me. I don't know why I thought it was impossible."

"Oh, they'll talk, all right," Rose told him, going over to look at the screen. "Harvey will bend the senator's ear all night long, telling him what a great idea it would be for Bethlehem to have its own professional soccer team. Right, Jack?"

But Jack Chatham wasn't paying attention to his mother; he was looking at the guest list Henry had projected onto the screen. "Hey, this thing's showing that there're over three hundred and fifty people on that list. I thought we'd agreed to keep it to a hundred and fifty on each side. What's going on?"

"Calm down, Jack," his mother commanded. "Hank and I added a few people, that's all."

"Oh really? And who's going to pay for all those extra people?"

Gloria, knowing that she had planned to purchase new slipcovers and drapes for the living room so that the photographs taken before the ceremony would have a pleasing background, found her voice. "Mom, I think you might have thought to consult us before you did this," she suggested mildly, so mildly that Elizabeth knew her mother was close to tears.

"You got that in one, Gloria," her husband said as Nick looked at his prospective father-in-law and noticed that the man's ears looked unusually red. "Well, I'm not paying for them, so you can just push whatever button's on that crazy thing that erases people."

Henry stood up. "There's no need for that, Jack. I'll gladly cover the additional expense."

Knowing Henry had just said exactly the wrong thing, no matter how well meant, Elizabeth felt the urge to duck her head and cover her ears as she waited for the explosion that was sure to come. She didn't have long to wait.

"The hell you will! And it's not the expense; it's the principle of the thing!" Jack exploded, his injured pride overwhelming his normally pleasant disposition. "Gloria, go tell the children to get upstairs to their rooms. Henry, we're going to have this out here and now. That's *my* daughter over there, and I'm the father of the bride. *I* make the plans. You got that?''

Henry, fortunately, ''got that,'' and quickly agreed, knowing that he had allowed himself to be caught up in Rose's schemes without taking the time to think of the consequences. Even if he hadn't realized it, one look at his son's face would have been enough to show him the error of his ways. Nick, he could see, was angry—very angry.

Unfortunately Rose wasn't as easily convinced. She loved her son, she really did, but she had always thought he was just a little too stubborn for his own good—she couldn't imagine who he took after, for *she* was certainly a most flexible person.

''Now see here, Jack,'' she began, standing in front of her son and poking a finger into his chest, ''I told you a dozen times that I want to contribute to this wedding, so climb down off that high horse of yours and let me help. This is a party—we're supposed to be able to look back on Elizabeth's wedding day and know that it was the best darn party anyone ever had!''

''Rose, I think—'' Henry began carefully.

''Mom, I said no, and I meant—'' Jack broke in.

''Mom? Can't you do anything?'' Elizabeth pleaded.

"Oh, wow!" John and Paul said together, standing in the archway.

"I said *no*!" Jack reiterated, and he reached down a hand and pushed several buttons on the computer at random, sending the screen to black.

"Now you've done it!" Henry shouted, rushing to save his latest "baby." "You've erased everything we've done. We'll have to start from scratch!"

"Not with me around, you won't," Nick said through clenched teeth, picking up his coat from the back of a nearby chair and slamming out the front door, forgetting to say goodnight to his fiancée.

"Isn't he masterful!" Megan gushed, standing in the archway, clutching a damp dishcloth to her breasts.

Elizabeth looked at the people who were left in the room, then at the closed front door, her eyes wide, her throat working silently. She spread her hands as if to comment on the bloody carnage that had been left behind by a rampaging army and then, her face crumpling as the tears she had been holding back threatened to fall, wailed, "Look what you've done! You've ruined *everything*!" before running for the stairs, sobbing, a hand to her mouth.

"Well," Gloria observed, hands on hips, clearly

taking charge of the shambles, "I hope you're all feeling proud of yourselves. Children, go back where you were, please. Jack, shake hands with Henry and apologize for breaking his little computer. Mother Chatham? What do you have to say for yourself?"

The silence in the living room after Gloria finished speaking was deafening. Rose Chatham dug the toe of her shoe into a corner of the aged oriental rug, averting her eyes from everyone else in the room. "Bridal nerves," she muttered quietly at last, knowing that Elizabeth was normally the most levelheaded person in the world and that most of what had gone wrong tonight could be laid squarely at her, Rose's, door. "That's all it is. Don't make a fuss, Gloria. She'll be fine in the morning."

"Nick, too," Henry put in after nervously clearing his throat. "He never did like scenes."

Jack put his arm around his wife's shoulders, feeling the tenseness in her slight body. "It's not like they're mad at each other, honey."

"No," Gloria agreed in her soft voice, "you're right. They're angry with us. And you know what—I don't blame them. I don't blame either one of them a bit. They aren't children; they're adults, and we're treating them as if they were babies. From now on, this wedding is strictly Elizabeth and

Nick's, and we are going to keep *our* noses out of it. Is that understood?''

Gloria Chatham didn't become angry often, but when she did, Jack Chatham—and even Rose— knew it was better to listen to her. Henry Lancaster took his cue from them.

''Agreed,'' they promised together, not noticing that Rose had crossed her fingers behind her back.

The day after Thanksgiving—called Black Friday in the retailing world—was traditionally the busiest shopping day of the year, and this Black Friday was even worse than usual. Shoppers descended on Lancaster's main downtown store an hour before the doors opened, eager to snatch up the early-bird specials, and Elizabeth had instructed her sales personnel to stand back and let the customers loose in the department for the first few minutes; she was fearful the clerks would be trampled by the stampeding horde.

Two hours after the store opened for business, Elizabeth surrendered the cash register that she had been working to Judy Holland and escaped to her office to catch her breath, knowing that she was going to explode the next time a customer asked her a silly question.

''Why don't you salespeople smile more? I should ask to see your manager,'' her last customer had complained just moments after the woman had slammed a heavy roasting pan down on the counter in front of three other customers who had been patiently waiting in line, insisting she had been there first.

Slumping into her chair, Elizabeth slipped off her shoes and lifted her feet to rest them on top of her desk, knowing she should never have worn high heels today. "That just goes to show me where my head is," she lamented, rubbing the back of her neck as her aching head continued to throb. "I can't believe I actually cried myself to sleep last night."

Elizabeth closed her eyes, remembering the events of the previous night. What an awful, terrible scene! And what a stupid, childish reaction! She still couldn't believe the way she had dissolved into tears, like a child, like Megan. "No," she corrected aloud, "Megan wouldn't be so silly. Why did Nick have to storm out that way? Talk about a rat deserting a sinking ship."

"I agree," came a voice from the doorway. "Personally, I think he should be flogged."

"Nick!" Elizabeth exclaimed, swiveling her chair around to see him standing half in, half out of her office, a huge bouquet of long-stemmed red roses held out in front of him. "Are those supposed to be a peace offering?"

Looking down at the flowers, Nick remarked, "Well, I don't think they'd make much of a shield, do you? How are you this morning? I didn't sleep all night."

He looked so vulnerable standing there that Elizabeth's heart, which had never really hardened against him, melted, and she got up and rushed into his arms. "Oh, Nick, what happened? How did it all get so crazy?"

Holding her tightly against his chest, Nick rubbed his cheek against the top of her head. "I'm not sure, darling, but I think it may have to do with something I asked you one day in Central Park."

Elizabeth rested her cheek against his chest. "What a wonderful day that was. It seems a lifetime ago. We should have stayed in New York and found a justice of the peace and avoided all this craziness. What fools we were."

Cupping her face in his hands, Nick tilted her head back so that he could look straight down into her wide brown eyes. "The worst is over, darling. I had it straight from my father's mouth this morning. He was waiting for me when I came to work, all hangdog looking and with profound apologies. Not only that, but he told me your mother made everyone promise to leave us alone."

Smiling, Elizabeth said, "Megan told me as much this morning before I left for work. According to my sister, my mother lined them all up like naughty children and bawled them out. I wish I could have been there.''

"But you weren't, were you?" Nick said softly. "Dad told me you ran to your bedroom, crying, right after I left. That's my fault, too, isn't it?"

Elizabeth closed her eyes and shook her head. "No, it was my fault. I've read about the way brides seem to dissolve into tears at the slightest provocation, but I didn't believe it until I found myself facedown on my bed, sobbing my heart out. I figured it was going to happen sooner or later, what with all this rush to have everything done on time.''

"Like the seating chart," Nick said, sitting in Elizabeth's chair and drawing her down on his lap. "Do you realize that we haven't even gotten the responses back from the invitations we sent? For all we know Aunt Margaret may be going to the Bahamas for Christmas and Senator Billings might be in Timbuktu. Why were they working on the seating chart now in the first place?''

"Gammy," Elizabeth said, as if that explained everything and, unfortunately, it did. Elizabeth loved her grandmother, loved her dearly, but the woman was going to drive her crazy. "Do you know what I found in my room this morning,

Nick? A sixpence! She wants me to put it in my shoe before I go down the aisle.''

''I like her,'' Nick declared firmly. ''She's done wonders for my father. I haven't seen him this happy since Mother died. Good Lord, I just thought of something—do you think they'll make a match of it?''

''Don't look so thrilled, darling,'' Elizabeth warned. ''We won't be able to pay them back by planning *their* wedding for them. Gammy already talked to me about your father and herself, and she told me that they're just good friends. Gammy and your father have both loved only one person in their lives, and they're content with their memories.''

''That's rather nice.''

''Yes,'' Elizabeth agreed, ''it is. Unless you know, as I do, that Gammy says she and your father plan to spend a lot of time together in the future—'raising hell' is the term she used, I think.''

Nick threw back his head and laughed, nearly toppling the two of them onto the floor. ''Elizabeth, what do you say we move to Arizona after the wedding?''

''Arizona? Lancaster's doesn't have any stores out there.''

''I'll *build* one,'' Nick bargained, pretending

desperation. "Single-handedly, brick by brick, if I have to. Elizabeth—marry me and take me away from all this!"

"You idiot!" Elizabeth laughed at his joke until, without warning, the atmosphere in the room changed, becoming supercharged with the knowledge that they were alone together, and in harmony once again. "Nick?" she asked tentatively.

"Hmm?" he answered vaguely, his gaze centered on the hint of cleavage he could see above the front closure of her blouse.

"Let's not ever fight." Elizabeth's voice was low, and deadly earnest. "I hate it. I was so lonely without you, without knowing that everything was still all right between us."

Raising his gaze to her face, Nick saw a hint of tears in her eyes and felt a lump in his own throat. "We'll never fight, darling," he vowed fervently, "and that's a promise."

Their lips met gently, tentatively; the kiss was one of healing, but passion quickly turned it to one of increasing fervor and intimacy. Their bodies shifted, hands moving hungrily over arms, shoulders, backs—striving for a closeness denied them by both the swivel chair and their location just a few feet away from the busy sales floor—until they reluctantly separated.

Elizabeth continued to cling to Nick as he

helped her to her feet, protesting, "I don't want you to leave. Can't you just lock the door?"

"As I believe I've said before, lady, you sure know how to pick your times and places," Nick joked, wishing he could lock the door and allow them to give way to their feelings. "Unfortunately we both have work to do. Now unhand me, woman, and let me out of here."

Holding on to his jacket lapels, Elizabeth cajoled, "Only if you promise to take me to lunch."

Nick looked at his watch, seeing that it was almost noon. "I don't have time for the store restaurant today, darling, so it will have to be hot dogs and potato chips at the snack bar. Is that all right?"

"Purest ambrosia," Elizabeth assured him, already putting on her shoes. She grabbed her purse and ran ahead to open the office door, promising, "I'll even let you pick up the check!" So saying, she bowed, flourishing her hand as if to invite him to precede her through the door.

Nick loved her, and all was right in Elizabeth's world once more.

Chapter Nine

Elizabeth sighed contentedly and rested her head against the back of the leather seat, lazily observing the familiar passing scenery as Nick steered the car along the deserted country road.

Sunday afternoons had become her favorite time. It was then that they spent their precious few hours alone together, and the peace and privacy they found inside his car seemed to be the only sanity left in a world gone mad.

Despite all Gloria's good intentions and warnings, life had not become easier for Nick and Elizabeth, even if their families were doing their best to be cooperative. Cooperation couldn't deliver seven bridesmaids' gowns to the bridal shop so that Elizabeth would stop having nightmares about going down the aisle behind attendants dressed in lovely gold-mesh-and-pearl snoods, gold leather high-heeled shoes—and their full-length crinolines.

All the good intentions in the world couldn't locate a single transportation service large enough to fit their needs, and Nick had spent two days calling rental agencies before he had found enough matching limousines for the entire wedding party.

Following a sample checklist in one of the books she had purchased, Elizabeth had already checked with the club manager about the menu, set up an appointment for her formal portrait, conferred with both bands about their selections, personally selected the silk flowers for the entire wedding party, hosted a bridesmaids' luncheon, finalized the seating chart and visited her doctor for a complete physical.

She had done all this while working long pre-Christmas hours at the store and trying, usually in vain, to find a few precious minutes alone with Nick, who was just as busy as she was. Many evenings Nick would come over to her parents' house after waiting for the sales figures from all the Lancaster store branches to be phoned in to his office, just in time to watch the eleven o'clock news with her and her father and then fall asleep on the floor with his head in her lap. She'd sit in the darkened living room with him for a while after her father went up to bed, stroking the hair back along his forehead, then reluctantly shoo him out the door, his sleepy good-night kiss usually landing somewhere to the left of her ear.

For all the romance we've been having lately, Elizabeth thought as she stole a look at Nick sitting behind the steering wheel, *we might as well be an old married couple. I wonder if he's becoming bored with me already?* As if the thought conjured up the words, she asked, "Nick? Wouldn't you want to drive to some secluded place—like maybe your apartment—so we can be alone? After all, we haven't seen each other since Friday."

Nick looked at her quickly out of the corner of his eye, just as if he were on a busy highway and couldn't really afford to take his attention off the road, and said, "We had lunch together yesterday, darling, remember? I'm sorry I couldn't stop by last night, but Dick Saunders and a couple of the guys from marketing insisted I join them for a drink for old times' sake. You know, sort of a goodbye drink. It got kind of late, so I just went home."

Elizabeth folded her arms across her stomach, her chin raised defiantly. "Old times' sake? My goodness, Nick, you're getting married—not going out of their lives forever. Why do you men always act like the groom is a condemned man, getting ready to walk the last mile? Besides, what does that have to do with our going back to your apartment? We've been driving around for almost an hour. I *know* I've seen that cow over there before."

Nick looked at the dashboard clock. "Yes, we have, haven't we? Good. Tell you what, darling, let's go visit Dad. It's Mrs. Gillespie's day off and he might be lonely."

Elizabeth liked Henry Lancaster, she liked him very much, but she wasn't in the mood for a quiet Sunday visit with the man, and she said as much to Nick. "You don't want to be alone with me, do you, Nicholas?" she added, frost edging her voice.

Turning back onto the highway, Nick, his strong jaw set belligerently, countered, "You sound like a wife, Elizabeth. Don't read so much into things, for pete's sake. I want to visit my father—so sue me!"

Elizabeth's right foot began beating a steady tattoo on the floor of the car. "Well, I don't! And I don't need a house to fall on me; you don't want to be alone with me. You probably would be happier watching a football game with some of your bachelor friends. Well, far be it from me to disappoint you. Nick, take me home!" *What is the matter with me?* Elizabeth wondered. *I'm acting like a nagging fishwife.*

Pounding a fist against the steering wheel a single time in frustration, Nick exclaimed, "*Women!* I *told* them this wouldn't work. I told them it was a stupid idea. But would they listen to me? No! Of course not! Of course I want to be alone with you, Elizabeth. I want it so bad I hurt! But in the gospel according to your grandmother, grooms are not to reason why, grooms are just to do and die. The whole thing is so damn stupid. I mean, why couldn't they just tell you? After all, it's *your* shower—" Nick slapped the side of his head with the palm of his hand. "Oh, damn! I blew it!"

Elizabeth gasped inaudibly, trying not to believe what she had just heard. She was *so* ashamed! Slinking down on the seat, as if she somehow could shrink into a smaller size—one less liable to be observed by a world that would point its collective finger at her and say, "There she is! That's the one! She blew it!" Elizabeth squeaked, "My *bridal shower*? Oh."

Pushing his hand through his hair in exasperation, Nick shook his head in disbelief at his own stupidity. Then slowly, he began to laugh, at first silently, and then with more abandon. "Yes, that's it, darling—*oh*. I was supposed to keep you away from both our houses until your family could leave for the party and all the guests had arrived safely at my dad's."

"It almost worked," Elizabeth provided soothingly, reaching out to touch his arm. "It would have worked—if I hadn't been such a pigheaded idiot."

"Yes, well," Nick temporized, "it's a good thing nobody ever whispered the secret of the H-bomb in my ear or it would be all over page one of every newspaper in the country by now. I can't believe I told you! Now what do we do? Everyone worked so hard to make the party a surprise."

"I'll just have to pretend that I'm surprised," Elizabeth said, wondering how she'd ever be able to fool her grandmother, who had been able to see straight through her all her life. "Don't worry, darling, I won't let anyone know you gave it all away."

Nick pulled the car into the long curved driveway that fronted on his father's house and turned off the engine. "I thought we were going to share the blame. How did it all get to be my fault?"

"Dick Saunders and his 'farewell' drink," Elizabeth answered with a smile, knowing she was being extremely female, and loving every minute of it. She leaned over to give him a kiss before he got out of the car. "After all, it seems only fair."

Two days later Megan was sitting on Elizabeth's canopy bed, helping her address thank-you notes for the bridal shower guests. "I can't believe you got three blenders, Liz. What are you going to do with them?"

Sitting cross-legged on the floor, Elizabeth sorted through her personal address book looking for an address. "I already returned two of them to the store and exchanged them for a waffle iron. Nick loves waffles and strawberry jam. Can you believe Gammy, Megan—giving me that gorgeous peignoir? The lace on the bodice actually matches my wedding gown. She's so wonderful. I can't imagine where she ever found it."

Megan licked another envelope before replying. "Yeah, it was pretty, but I liked the baby-doll nightgown us bridesmaids gave you. All that black see-through lace—and those red bows—wow! You should have seen yourself, Liz. You got *so* red when we passed it around the room and Aunt Margaret held it up to the light to check the seams and said there was more thread there than in the whole gown."

Megan was silent for a moment, then changed the subject, bringing it around to herself—a subject of unending interest to her. "Liz, may I ask you a question? Now remember, you *have* to tell me the truth. Do you think I'm pretty?"

Elizabeth heard the words and allowed them to repeat themselves inside her head, clearing away the zip code for Manhattan that she had almost remembered without looking it up again in the directory. How should she answer that question?

A year ago, even six months ago, she could have teased, "Fishing for compliments, again. Megan?" and gotten away with it. But not now. Not since Nick. Elizabeth may have been living in her own world most of the time since her engagement, but that didn't mean she hadn't seen the changes taking place in her seventeen-year-old sister. She was sure Megan had a case of hero worship for Nick and while it was rather cute, it was also a very delicate situation, one that needed special handling.

"Pretty, Megan?" she answered her sister at last. "I guess that depends. What kind of pretty are we talking about here?"

Megan pulled a pained face. "Well, I certainly don't mean pretty as in Aunt Margaret pinching my cheeks and gushing, 'Isn't she a pretty little pudding?' I mean, do you think I appeal to men?"

Elizabeth leaned back against the base of her dresser and looked at her sister through narrowed eyes, "Men, Meg? Don't you mean boys?"

Pushing the thank-you cards to one side, Megan hopped to her feet and began pacing back and forth in the bedroom. "*Boys,* Lizzie? Oh, cut me a break! John and Paul are *boys.* I have nothing in common with *boys.*" She stopped in the middle of the room and turned to face her sister, dramatically tossing her head. "Did I tell you that I plan to become a writer?"

"A writer? Really? Isn't that wonderful! You're growing up, Megan. I had no idea you'd been seriously thinking about your future. But what does becoming a writer have to do with whether or not you're pretty enough to appeal to boys—I mean, *men*?"

Megan sighed in exasperation, unable to believe her intelligent older sister could be so dense. "Look, Liz," she explained patiently, "how do you expect me to learn anything about the world—about *life*—if I don't get to know some men?"

"When you say men, Meg, do you mean men who have been around a bit—men like Nick?"

"Oh, Liz," Megan gushed, throwing herself back down on the bed so that Elizabeth scrambled to remove the thank-you cards before they were bent, "you *do* understand. Nick is, well, Nick is so *smooth,* you know, so *sexy*. He makes Billy Perkins look like a baby."

"Billy Perkins. Isn't he the boy who asked you to the Sophomore Sweetheart Dance last year?"

Megan rolled her eyes. "Yes, isn't it dreadful? I mean, really—I'm a writer! I'm going to write for Nick, aren't I? What could I possibly have in common with a *football player?*"

Elizabeth rubbed a weary hand across her eyes. "Oh, brother," she said under her breath, "now what?'' Megan was at such a sensitive age, and it appeared that she had chosen Nick for her first grown-up crush. He'd have to be careful.

"Anyway, Liz," Megan went on, oblivious of her sister's fears, holding up her head so that her throat would appear longer, more willowy, like the heroine in the novel she had just finished, "you haven't answered my question. Am I pretty?"

Looking back at her sister, Elizabeth felt her heart melt. "Pretty, Megan? Darling, you're beautiful! Just please, give yourself some time. You have a lot of years ahead of you to break hearts."

"I know," Megan told her happily, picking up a pen and starting to copy another address, "but I have to start *sometime,* don't I?"

"She's got a crush on *who!* Elizabeth, that's crazy. You must have read the situation wrong. For crying out loud, Megan is only seventeen."

Elizabeth was sitting in Nick's office, taking a break from the sales floor to ask his help with her sister. "I think that's *whom,* but I guess that isn't really important now. Look, Nick, I know I must sound ridiculous to you, but believe me, the girl is serious. Oh, I should have seen it coming, but I didn't. I mean, first you help her with that fashion feature for her school paper, and then you treat her like she's all grown up—"

"How the hell am I supposed to treat her?" Nick broke in, still confused. "She's not a pig-tailed baby."

"Don't remind me," Elizabeth said, sighing. "Megan has very patiently explained to me that she's grown way beyond mere boys; she's only attracted to *men* now."

Nick sank back into his chair behind the desk. "Hey, you aren't kidding, are you? Great! As if we didn't have enough problems. Now what do we do?"

Elizabeth got up and walked around the desk, to stand behind his chair and slide her arms around his chest. "Well, I guess you could always dump me and run off to Maryland with Megan," she suggested, bending her head to nibble at the side of his neck.

Nick was quiet for a few moments, then said consideringly, "Yes, there's always that, of course. I should have thought of it myself. But you'd probably sue me for breach of contract. I have a feeling you might be nasty that way. Still, Megan is quite pretty."

"Wretch!" Elizabeth exclaimed, nipping his neck with her teeth. "I think I'm marrying a dirty old man. Now, be serious. We have to do something. You know, I had expected Megan to be jealous of you—because you're taking me away from her—but I guess she got over that separation business when I moved to New York. Nick? What is it? You're looking suddenly smug. Have you thought of something!''

Nick answered happily, "Not some*thing,* darling, some*one.* My mother's youngest sister's son, Mike. He's a junior in college and one of the ushers. You and I thought he could be with your cousin Lisa, but we'll have him partner your sister instead. As I remember Mike, he's quite handsome—broad shoulders and all that. He'll get Megan's attention, don't you think? Feel free to kiss me, darling, right after you say thank you very much.''

Elizabeth bit her knuckle as Nick held out his cheek for her kiss. "Not so fast, Nick. Don't you think we'd just be trading one problem for another?''

"Darling, Mike lives in Maine and goes to college in California. Megan can write to him after the wedding, it'll be good practice for her if she wants to make writing her career. And in the meantime, we can show her what a good, solid marriage we have.''

Elizabeth congratulated him, leaning forward to kiss him on the end of his nose. "What an absolutely brilliant idea! Tell me, how did I ever get so lucky? I'm marrying a genius. Kiss me, Albert.''

"Albert?"

"Albert. As in Einstein. A real genius."

Nick lifted his head and pulled Elizabeth's face down to him. "Yes, I am aren't I? Come closer, woman. Oh, dammit, now what?" Nick hit the intercom button and growled, "Marge? I thought I told you I didn't want to be disturbed?"

"Yes, sir," Marge's voice said through the chocolate-brown box, "but it's Ms. Chatham's grandmother on the phone. She says it's urgent."

"I'll take it, Nick," Elizabeth said, already reaching for the telephone. "Gammy, is that you? What's wrong? Is someone ill?"

Nick shook his head and laughed. "Why is it women always think somebody's sick?" he asked the room in general before sobering, as Elizabeth's face had suddenly gone white. "Elizabeth?" he whispered. "What is it?"

"Uh-huh, uh-huh," Elizabeth was saying, shushing Nick with a shooing motion of her hand, "I understand. Well, can he walk? What? Oh— well, that's something, I guess. Okay, Gammy, thanks for calling. I'll be home for supper. Tell John I hope he feels better."

Watching as Elizabeth replaced the receiver, Nick could barely contain his curiosity. "So? What's wrong with John? It is John, isn't it?"

Elizabeth walked around to the front of the desk and collapsed into a chair. "I've got some good news and some bad news, as the joke goes. Which do you want first?''

''Either one. You choose,'' Nick said, relaxing a bit as he saw that Elizabeth was smiling—even it if wasn't a very big smile.

''The bridesmaids' gowns have finally come in,'' she told him. ''So the girls won't be going down the aisle in their underwear.''

Nick grinned at her, waggling his eyebrows. ''There goes another fantasy straight to hell—so, what's the good news?''

Trying to look stern, Elizabeth's eyes betrayed her amusement. ''The *bad* news is—John broke his foot in gym class this morning. He's in a cast up to his knee. Mom just called Gammy from the hospital to tell her.''

Nick was all concern. ''You want to go home? I can arrange cover for you?''

Elizabeth rubbed the side of her cheek while she mentally pictured John clomping down the aisle on crutches. ''No, that's all right. This is John's third broken bone, if I remember correctly. Paul's already broken his wrist—and an ankle, I think. Our family doctor always jokes that the Chathams have personally paid for his new X-ray machine. Mom is used to it by now.''

The thought that Elizabeth had already considered finally registered with Nick. ''Good Lord, how's John supposed to wear a tux? He'll never get the pants over the cast. Elizabeth, my offer still stands—if we leave now we can be in Maryland by dinnertime.''

It was strange, but seeing the usually unflappable Nick flustered, Elizabeth suddenly became very calm. She got up and walked around the desk to stand behind Nick, massaging his shoulders. ''Now who's suffering from prewedding nerves? Gammy says John will be on crutches for a week and then they'll fit him with a walking cast. I think I've already figured out a way we can keep him in the wedding, so don't worry, darling. John's cast should be the least of our worries. Now,'' she asked, leaning down to kiss his earlobe, ''where were we before we were so rudely interrupted?''

Five minutes later the intercom buzzed again, reminding Nick of a meeting he had planned with his merchandise coordinators, and Elizabeth returned to the housewares department.

Saints Simon and Jude Church wasn't one of the oldest buildings in Bethlehem but it was one of the most impressive, Nick decided as he parked his car and made his way across Broad Street in the late afternoon traffic.

A massive building of hand-hewed gray and brown stone, its twin towers rose high into the sky and the large, intricately traced nave window, carved in limestone in the Gothic style, rose above statues of the two saints that surrounded the double front oak doors.

Once inside, Nick stood at the rear of the church, looking down the hundred-foot aisle at the three massive Gothic wood rear altars that stood against the stone wall. In the near darkness he could make out the wood trusses on the three-story-high ceiling and it reminded him of churches he had seen years earlier on a trip to England. He squinted slightly, imagining the brilliant colors that sunlight would produce inside the church as it flowed through the two dozen blue-and-red-mosaic stained-glass windows that pierced the stone walls.

He was early, and no one else had arrived, giving him time to walk down the aisle, conscious of the echo his footsteps made in the cavernous interior. Approaching the main central altar, he admired its black marble front inlaid with deeply carved white marble in the design of vines and grapes, twin carvings of two peacocks balancing the whole.

It was a beautiful church; but now, decorated for the Christmas Season, it was glorious. The three rear altars were adorned with massive red and white poinsettia plants, unadorned Christmas trees lined the stone walls three deep and there were dozens of ornate brass candle holders scattered around the entire altar area.

It was the perfect setting for a Christmas wedding.

A sound at the back of the church brought Nick's attention away from the pleasant daydream he was having: a mental vision of himself standing at the altar rail as Elizabeth, a vision in white lace and satin, her face hidden behind a gossamer veil, floated down the aisle to take his outstretched hand.

"Hi, Nick," Megan said cheerily, coming down the aisle holding a paper plate covered with pink and white and blue bows. "How do you like my flowers? Crazy, huh? Each bridesmaid—and Liz, of course—is going to carry pretend bouquets we made out of the bows that came on her shower presents. Gammy says it's traditional, but I think she made it up, just to keep me busy during the party and away from the onion dip."

Nick nodded in reply, but he wasn't really paying attention. Looking over Megan's shoulder he asked anxiously, "Where's your sister? I called her office but her assistant said she'd already left. I want to get this rehearsal over with."

Megan laughed. "Nervous, Nick? Relax, it's only pretend. The real thing doesn't happen for three whole days. Did I tell you that your father brought your cousin Mike over to meet me? We're going to the movies together tomorrow afternoon. Oh—here she comes. Darn it, Gammy's with her. She promised to stay home out of the way. Father Chuck doesn't stand a chance; Gammy will be giving orders right and left, just you wait and see. She would have made a great mother superior.''

Elizabeth was walking toward him now, wearing the flowing mohair cape that she had worn that day in Central Park. She held a mass of white bows and streamers in her hands. Her face was bright, yet somehow solemn, and he imagined that her mind was now working along the same lines as his had been a few minutes earlier. He didn't know why, but it made him feel better. "Hello, darling,'' he said as she joined him, kissing her lightly on the cheek. "Are you ready for our rehearsal?''

Elizabeth only nodded, unable to speak. She'd been attending Saints Simon and Jude since she was a child…so why hadn't she ever realized before just how *long* the aisle was? How was she ever going to get down that aisle without tripping, or stepping on her gown, or dissolving into tears like a baby? This big wedding business was insane—how had she ever allowed herself to be talked into it?

Nick took her hand, noticing that it was ice-cold. "Elizabeth? Darling? Are you all right? I think everyone else is here now, in the rear of the church, but if you want to sit down for a moment, I don't think anyone would mind.''

''I—I—''

''All right, boys and girls! Father Chuck, everyone is here now, so let's get this show on the road.'' Rose Chatham walked briskly down the aisle, clapping her hands to gain everybody's attention. ''Elizabeth, get to the back of the church to make your entrance. Jack, go with her, you're the father of the bride, you know. Nick, good to see you. Now go away. You don't belong out here until the music starts. Now, if you please, Father? Anytime you're ready.''

The priest raised his eyes to the vaulted roof and—at least Nick thought so—sent up a silent prayer before addressing the bridesmaids and ushers about their duties iin the processional, concluding his instructions by saying, ''If that's all right with you, Mrs. Chatham?''

Luckily it was, and the rest of the rehearsal went off smoothly, a fact that worried Rose, who had always heard that a good rehearsal meant a bad opening night. When Elizabeth reminded her that this was a wedding, not a Broadway show, Rose only sniffed, then went off with Henry Lancaster to make sure everything was in place for the rehearsal dinner at a nearby restaurant.

Just before the meal was served, Rick Jamieson, Nick's college roommate and best man, stood to make the traditional toast to the prospective bride and groom. Holding his glass high, Rick turned to the guests of honor and said, "Elizabeth and Nick, as you stand on the brink of committing matrimony, let me quote to you the words of the illustrious Benjamin Franklin: 'Keep your eyes wide open before marriage, half shut afterwards.'"

"What's that supposed to mean, Rick?" Nick asked, laughing.

Rick pulled a face, winking at Elizabeth. "Darned if I know, old man, but it sounded good, didn't it?"

"I have a better one," Rose said from her place halfway down the table, and the entire party rose for another toast. "To my darling Elizabeth and her Nick. 'A new commandment I give unto you, That ye *love* one another,' the Gospel according to John."

"Amen," Henry whispered, draining his glass.

Chapter Ten

Elizabeth leaned over and looked at the alarm clock. Eight in the morning. The wedding wasn't until three o'clock. What was she supposed to do with herself in the meantime? Oh, why couldn't she sleep!

She had a hairdresser's appointment at noon, but she certainly didn't have to get up at eight o'clock. Besides, her stomach hurt; it felt tight, like someone had tied her insides up in knots.

The weather! She had forgotten about the weather. She'd watched every major television station's weather report last night and two of them had forecast snow. How was she to keep the hem of her gown dry if it was snowing? What if it snowed so much that half the guests didn't make it to the ceremony? Whoever heard of getting married in the middle of winter in Pennsylvania! Why did she think June weddings were so popular?

Throwing back the covers, Elizabeth dived through the draperies she had pulled around the four-poster bed and ran, barefoot, to the window. Pushing aside the curtain, she looked out, then leaned her forehead against the bitter cold pane. It was all right. The sun was shining. How could she have been so worried? Everyone knew television weathermen didn't know what they were talking about!

"Elizabeth? I thought I heard you moving around up here. May I come in?"

"Mom!" Elizabeth exclaimed, turning to see her mother standing in the door, a lap tray in her hands. "Oh, you brought me breakfast. How wonderful. But I couldn't eat a thing, honestly."

"Nonsense," Gloria scoffed, clicking out the tray's collapsible legs and motioning for Elizabeth to climb back under the covers. "I've only brought you some tea and toast. You have to keep up your strength. Nervous, darling?"

Pressing her lips together tightly, Elizabeth nodded. Suddenly without warning, she felt close to tears. This was the last morning she and her mother would have alone together in this room. Everything was so final now, everything was the last thing, being done for the last time. "I—I guess it's another case of bridal nerves. Silly, isn't it?"

After positioning the tray across her daughter's lap, Gloria sat down on the edge of the high bed. "Oh, I don't know, Elizabeth. I think I can remember feeling a bit nervous myself, all those years ago. There's something so final about getting married, isn't there?"

Now Elizabeth nodded vigorously, happy her mother understood. "I love Nick, honestly I do, but—"

"But marriage is a big step and you can't help but have some last-minute doubts," Gloria finished for her. "That's perfectly natural. You two only met a few months ago. But you've got a level head, Elizabeth, and I know you've thought this all out carefully."

Talking around a bite of toast, Elizabeth countered, "But have I, Mom? I mean, maybe I just fell in love with love. I mean, I'm twenty-six years old, and God knows Gammy thought I was on my way to becoming an old maid—so what if I just convinced myself that I was in love because I was afraid I'd never meet the right man?"

"Oh, my," Gloria responded, looking closely at her daughter, "you do have yourself in quite a tizzy, don't you? So you were getting desperate, and Nick is just the male body who happened along at the right moment? Do you really think that's what happened, Elizabeth?''

Elizabeth's chin fell against her chest. ''It sounds pretty silly when you say it like that, doesn't it?''

Gloria reached out a hand to gently stroke her daughter's hair. ''Nick Lancaster is a wonderful man, darling, and he loves you very much. We can see it in his eyes every time he looks at you, just as we see the love in your eyes when you look at him. Do you really think your father and I would allow you to marry Nick if we didn't think the marriage was right, in every way?''

Biting her lip to keep back her tears, Elizabeth shook her head. ''Gammy would laugh at me.''

''Your grandmother had me up half the night, giving me helpful hints on how to handle you this morning. She saw this coming, darling—you know your Gammy. Now she also gave me a detailed list of instructions for you. I have it here somewhere.''

Elizabeth laughed shakily, brushing away her tears with the back of her hands. ''That also sounds very much like Gammy. What does she say?''

Gloria reached into her apron pocket and pulled out a small piece of paper. ''Let's see, oh, yes— here we go. 'Elizabeth—get up at eight.' Well, she had that right, didn't she? 'Finish crying on mother's shoulder at eight-thirty; eat breakfast.' Honestly, that woman!''

''What next? I hope I don't have to do push-ups or anything.''

''No, the list gets pretty basic from here: the bridesmaids will arrive at one, already in their makeup, to get dressed, and there's a complete schedule for the bathroom this morning, so that all of us may take a shower without running out of hot water. You're first, darling, and you're supposed to take a long bubble bath.''

''That sounds delicious,'' Elizabeth remarked, brightening. ''Being first in the bathroom—ahead of John and Paul—is like a gift from heaven. I guess I'd better get to it, huh?''

Gloria folded the paper and returned it to her apron pocket. ''Are you sure you don't want me to drive you to the hairdresser? I'd still have plenty of time to dress when we got back.''

Elizabeth shook her head. ''No, I think I may need the time alone, if it's all right with you. Mom?'' she said as her mother moved to get off the bed.

''Yes, honey?''

''I love you, Mommy,'' Elizabeth whispered, her voice husky, reaching out her arms.

Gloria cradled her oldest daughter close, fighting

back a few tears of her own. "I love you, too, baby. I always will. Be happy."

He was numb. Completely numb. It was eleven o'clock in the morning and he was still sitting in the kitchen of his apartment, nursing his third cup of coffee and hoping that it would eventually make some impact on his brain.

It was ridiculous! Here he was, a man who was cool under fire, the victor in countless business confrontations—the man who had just three weeks earlier concluded a deal that would more than double the size of Lancaster, Inc. by annexing a large southern department-store chain—and he was having trouble remembering his best man's name!

Rick Jamieson sat across the table from his college friend, lazily waving his hand back and forth as if trying to see if Nick responded to stimuli. "Yo! Nick! You in there anywhere? Come out, come out, wherever you are."

Nick blinked twice, and swallowed the cold dregs lying in the bottom of his cup before pouring himself another cup from the decanter that sat on the table. "Yuk! Oh—Rick. What's the matter? Were you saying something?"

Rick, a psychologist, pulled at his earlobe, an unconscious habit he'd acquired while listening to his patients tell their life stories. "Yes, I was, as a matter of fact. I was asking you if Beth is romantically involved with anyone at the moment.''

''Beth?'' Nick didn't know what his friend was talking about. ''Who the hell is Beth?''

''Blond. Beautiful. Bridesmaid. Beth. Word association, Nick, word association. She's Elizabeth's maid of honor. Ring any bells now?''

Nick nodded. ''Beth's the one from New York, right? No, she's not involved with anyone—but she's a nice woman, Rick. She's not your usual love 'em and leave 'em type; she could get hurt. So watch it, okay?''

Rick stood up and carried his coffee cup over to the counter. ''Got it, old friend. I'll be good.'' He sat down again and looked across the table, wearing his professional, interested face. ''So—you want to talk about it?''

Sitting up straight, Nick looked at his friend warily. ''Talk about it? Talk about what? I don't know what you mean.''

Once again Rick tugged at his earlobe. ''You sure about that? I don't mean to pry, but you look like you just lost your last friend. I thought bridegrooms were supposed to be happy—or hungover—the morning of their wedding. I'd hate to think I gave up Christmas skiing in St. Moritz just to watch you jilt that pretty girl. *Are* you having second thoughts?''

"Second thoughts?" Rick had Nick's full attention now. "No. Why the hell would you think something like that? I love Elizabeth."

"Okay. Then maybe you can tell me this," his friend persisted, "since when do you put seven teaspoons of sugar in your coffee?"

Nick took a sip of coffee from his cup and shivered as the sickeningly sweet liquid assaulted his taste buds. "Good Lord! What's wrong with me? My mind's turned to mush!"

Rick leaned back in the kitchen chair, balancing it on its two back legs. "Well, normally I'd tell you to call my office for an appointment, but in your case I think I'll make an exception. You're scared, old friend. Scared right out of your socks."

"Of what? Elizabeth and I love each other. It's not like I'm afraid we're making a mistake. This marriage is right—for both of us."

"I'm not talking about that kind of scared," Rick corrected. "Tell me—when do you and I walk out of that side room and approach the altar?"

Nick's eyes shifted, avoiding his friend's interested gaze. "When the music starts—no, I didn't mean that. After Gloria is seated, right? But the ushers have to roll down the white runner first, don't they?" Nick buried his head in his hands. "I don't remember! Why don't I remember?"

Rick dug in his pocket and pulled out a folded sheet of paper. "I bow to a wisdom greater than mine," he said, unfolding the paper and shoving it across the table to Nick. "Mrs. Chatham handed me this last night. It's a complete list of everything you have to do today, up to leaving for the reception after the ceremony. If you look at it, you'll see that you're supposed to be shaving in—let's see here—fifteen minutes. Better get going, buddy."

Nick took one hand away from his eyes to pick up the paper, reading down the list slowly, and marveling at its completeness. "Rose," he said, shaking his head. "It's all here, every move I have to make. That woman never ceases to amaze me."

"Yeah," Rick agreed, helping his friend to his feet and guiding him toward the bathroom. "I've been thinking about her. You know, if everybody had a grandmother like that, it might just put me out of business. Or make me a millionaire," he added consideringly.

"Hey, Gammy!" John shouted loudly from the hallway. "The cake is here already."

"Hurray for the cake," Rose responded abstractedly from the dining room. "Now get back in here so I can figure out what to do with you—

the cake is where? Grab that delivery man, John, and don't let him leave!"

"What's going on, Mom?" Jack called down the steps as he saw his mother advancing down the hall with all the delicacy of a charging bull. "It sounds like there's a war on."

"I don't believe it," Rose was muttering under her breath. "I just don't believe it! If I told those people once, I told them a dozen times—*we* live on Spring Street, the *cake* goes to the country club! I tell you, it's true what they say, you just can't get good help these days— *You!* Hold it right there, young man, and come back here this instant," she called to the deliveryman, who was already halfway down the porch steps.

"You'll have to pick one, Mom," Jack pointed out from behind her. "I don't think he can hold it there and still come back here. And stop yelling at him, you're scaring the guy. It's really getting to you, isn't it, that everything isn't perfect after all your plans? You know what they say about the best laid plans, Mom."

"Hey, that's some cake, isn't it?" Paul said, joining the rest of them in the now crowded hallway. "Look at all those flowers glopped all over it. They're sugar, aren't they? Where's the little bride and groom dolls?"

Rose closed her eyes and began slowly counting

to ten. "One—I'll thank you, Jack, to stop grinning. Two—I'm not upset. Three—I never get upset. Four—John, go back into the dining room and try one more time to get those pants over that cast. Five—young man, this cake does not belong here. Please check your delivery slip. Six—Paul Chatham, if you lay so much as one finger on that icing I will personally break both your— *Now what?*"

Gloria hastened out of the living room to pick up the phone extension just inside the dining room. A few moments later she held her hand over the receiver and called out frantically: "It's the church housekeeper on the phone. Father Chuck is in the Emergency Room. They think he may have had a heart attack. Poor man, and he's so young! Now what do we do?"

Elizabeth, who was just returning from the hairdresser's, held open the front door as the delivery man staggered out under the weight of the cake. "What?" she asked as she closed the door behind her and leaned on it, her heart dropping to her toes. "Oh, no. Nick and I liked him so much. Now what are we supposed to do? Gammy?"

Seeing the panic in Elizabeth's eyes, the panic in all her family's eyes, Rose took a deep breath—and then took charge. Removing the phone from Gloria's nerveless fingers, she asked the person on the other end which emergency room the priest had been taken to, hung up, and then pulled out the telephone directory.

"What are you going to do, Mom?" Jack asked, leaning against the dining room archway. "Have the poor man paged in intensive care?"

Making a face at her son, Rose dialed the emergency room pretending to be Father Chuck's sister, and within five minutes had all the information she needed. "It was just a muscle spasm he got playing basketball this morning in the church hall. He's fine, and is already on his way back to the rectory," she was able to tell everyone as she hung up. "Honestly, you people get upset so easily. I tell you, it's a good thing you've got me around. Now, John, how do those pants fit?"

"I still can't get them over my cast, Gammy," he told her, balancing on one foot as he tried to pull the material over his plaster-encased lower leg. "You're going to have to split the seam some more, I guess."

The doorbell rang and, as John hopped into the kitchen on one foot so nobody could see him with his pants down around his knees, the front door opened, admitting four of the bridesmaids. "Elizabeth!" Jennifer exclaimed in delight. "Your hair looks wonderful! Gosh, I'm nervous! Hey, does Beth still own a little red compact with a bumper sticker on it that says 'I'd rather be skiing'? We passed a car like that on the thruway near Easton. It was pulled off on the shoulder with the hood up.''

Jack was already picking up his car keys. ''Gloria, do you want to go for a little ride? I think we could use a few minutes of peace and quiet. Mom? How does this fit into your little schedule?''

Rose stood in the dining room, slowly shaking her head. She couldn't understand it. She had planned everything, down to the last detail. How could it all be falling apart like a house of cards at the last minute? Then she remembered that it had bothered her that the rehearsal had gone so well, and she smiled at her son. ''Actually, Jack, I feel better now that we've hit a few snags. Now I know the ceremony will go off without a hitch. Well, don't just stand there gaping at me—get moving before that crazy Beth finds herself a good-looking man to fix her car for her. There's no room for another guest on the seating chart.''

The priest spread his arms, saying, ''And now, for the first time in public, let me present to you Mr. and Mrs. Nicholas Lancaster!''

Elizabeth felt Nick's warm hand squeezing hers tightly as they turned to face their guests, who were all on their feet in the pews, applauding. She could see her mother and father in the pew directly behind the bridesmaids, her mother leaning her head against her father's shoulder as he cradled her waist.

Gammy, she noticed, had been true to her word, and was sitting with Henry Lancaster, the two of them unashamedly wiping away happy tears in between their enthusiastic clapping.

She wasn't surprised to see that nearly everyone in the church was looking a bit misty-eyed. It had been a beautiful ceremony, from beginning to end. Elizabeth was now amazed that she had been nervous before; that she had stood at the rear of the church holding on to her father as if he could lend her some of his rocklike strength.

But the moment Jennifer, her matron of honor, had stepped onto the white cloth runner that led down the aisle and Elizabeth had caught her first glimpse of Nick waiting for her at the altar, all her fears had disappeared.

She had only been vaguely aware of the guests that stood on either side of her as she moved down the aisle, her entire world centering on the man who waited for her, his heart and his pride shining in his eyes. When her father had lifted her veil to give her a kiss she had smiled and said, "Goodbye, Daddy," bidding farewell to the life she had known, before taking another step forward and saying, "Hello, Nick," willingly embracing their future together.

And now it was over, the ceremony that had bound them together, tying silken chains around them that they were more than willing to bear. They stood together, looking out over their guests, their heads reeling with joy. Nick leaned toward her slightly and whispered facetiously, "We done good, wife, now let's get out of here!"

Still holding hands, they walked back down the aisle, never stopping until they reached the street and Nick helped Elizabeth into the waiting limousine. A chilled bottle of champagne awaited them there, and they lingered only until the rest of the bridal party were in their limousines before pulling away from the church and heading for the reception.

"I don't know why your grandmother insists on this, Liz," her father protested as he led Elizabeth onto the dance floor. "We already did all of this earlier. I danced with you, you danced with Henry, Nick danced with your mother—all God's children danced with everybody else. What are the two of us doing out here alone?"

Elizabeth was enjoying her father's discomfort. Never one to seek the limelight, he was uncomfortable enough in his tuxedo, without Gammy pulling one of her little stunts. "I don't know, Dad. She says it's one of her little 'extras.' You know, sometimes that woman absolutely scares me."

Just then the musicians—from both bands— struck up the music, and the strains of "Daddy's Little Girl" filled the room. "Oh, Dad," Elizabeth marveled, "it's the song you used to sing for me when I sat on your lap and you played the piano. I think I'm going to cry again."

Jack Chatham's eyes were none too dry, either, as he clasped his oldest daughter to him, his feet barely moving to the music as he rubbed his big hand clumsily, affectionately, up and down her back. Out of the corner of his eye, he could see his mother standing at one side of the dance floor, a broad smile on her face as she watched her son make a spectacle of himself by falling apart like a sentimental fool. "I love you, honey," he said gruffly just as he felt Nick tap him on the shoulder, rescuing him from the moment like a good son-in-law should. "Take good care of her, son," he warned gruffly before searching the crowd with his eyes, longing for the comfort of his wife's under-standing arms.

"Come on, Lizzie—wind up and wing it!" John yelled from the sidelines. Brothers were so en-couraging. Elizabeth waved to him, still marveling at how good he looked, dressed in his tuxedo jacket and a pair of black sweatpants that sported a hand-sewn strip of black satin down each side. Only the foot of the white cast poking out from the hem of the pants gave him away.

Elizabeth looked over her shoulder at the bridesmaids and guests who were waiting for her to throw her bouquet and gasped, "Gammy! What are you doing there?"

"I'm single, aren't I?" her grandmother quipped, and a few moments later, when Elizabeth turned around to see who had caught the specially made nosegay, the woman held it up triumphantly, saying, "Not so bad for an old lady, huh?"

When Nick threw the garter, Rick Jamieson caught it by leaping three feet into the air and snagging it with one finger. After he had slipped it on Rose's leg, to the accompaniment of cheerful hoots and suggestions, Elizabeth had slipped out of the room and made her way upstairs to change.

Gloria and Megan went with her, the rest of the bridesmaids graciously giving them a few minutes alone together as Elizabeth changed into her baby-pink wool suit and recombed her hair. "Everyone's enjoying themselves," she said, looking in the mirror to check her makeup. "I think it's a good time to slip away, don't you?"

Gloria was standing at the other side of the

room, taking great pains to hang the wedding gown just so, doing her best to keep busy. "Unless you want to listen to your grandmother's instructions on how to handle the honeymoon—yes, I think this is the perfect time. Megan, hand me that plastic bag. I want to cover the gown before something happens to it. You were a beautiful bride, Liz. Your father and I were so proud of you."

"Did you get a chance to talk to Mike, Liz? You know—Nick's cousin. Isn't he terrific! He says he's going to invite me to Maine this summer to visit his family."

Elizabeth turned from the mirror to smile at her sister. Nick's plan had worked. "Megan," she began, thinking that she had never seen her looking quite so grown-up. "I'm really going to miss those little talks we used to have in my room. Will you do me a favor?"

"Sure, Liz," Megan answered, taking her sister's hand. She didn't want to admit it, but she was going to miss those late-night talks herself. "Anything."

"Will you keep an eye on Gammy for me? She likes late-night talks, too, you know, and she's a great listener when you've got boy problems."

"Gammy?" Megan made a face. "She always says I'm still wet behind the ears. She'll laugh at me."

"No she won't," Elizabeth assured her. "She loves you very much—she loves all of us. In fact, now that she's got me settled, I wouldn't be the least surprised if she made you her next project."

"Really? Gee, I wish I could believe—"

"Megan!" Rose called loudly, entering the room. "What are you doing up here wasting time? Mike's downstairs, wandering around like a lost sheep. Go dance with him."

Megan looked at her sister and grinned. "Yes, Gammy," she said, giving her grandmother a kiss as she sped out of the room.

"And I expect you to come to my room tonight to tell me all about it," Rose called after her. "I'm an old lady; I have to get my thrills somehow. She's going to break a dozen hearts before she's through," she declared happily, looking at Gloria and Elizabeth. "Now, what do you two think you're doing—setting up a sewing circle? Nick's already waiting downstairs, champing at the bit and ready to leave. You'd better find him and get moving before Aunt Margaret spies him and you never get out of here."

"What's this?" Elizabeth asked, reaching down to pick up a small packet of brochures that were held together with a rubber band and that Nick had tossed onto the seat.

Nick turned the car onto the main highway, leaving the country club and all their wedding guests behind. "Oh, Rose handed that to me on our way out the door. It's a bunch of folders listing things to do in New York City. I think she's got every minute of our honeymoon planned, right down to which restaurants we should go to for dinner. Quite a woman, your grandmother."

Elizabeth laid her head on his shoulder and sighed. "I'm surprised you didn't strangle her on the spot. After all, I think we're capable of planning our own honeymoon."

"I am, at any rate," Nick told her, loosening his tie. "Darling, what would you say if I told you we aren't going to New York?"

Lifting her head to look at him in the darkness inside the car, she said slowly, "I think I'd say it was fine with me. But where are we going? I packed winter clothes, so I hope you aren't planning on someplace with a beach."

"Nope."

"Not going to tell me, are you?" Elizabeth asked, snuggling against him once more. "Does Gammy know about this?"

"Ah, that's the beauty of it, darling. *Nobody* knows about it. We're married now, and from now on, we'll make our own plans."

"Sounds heavenly," Elizabeth said. "So— where are we going?"

Nick grinned at her, obviously quite pleased with himself. "That, my dearest wife, is for me to know and you to find out!"

"Yes, the food was wonderful, Rose, thank you for recommending the restaurant. What? Oh, that's nice. We can use another silver platter. Who sent it? My Uncle William? It's a shame he couldn't come to the wedding; you would have liked him." Nick sat up slightly in the bed and adjusted the pillows at his back.

"I thought you were going to tell her we went to see the Statue of Liberty," Elizabeth whispered, her fingers slowly marching up his bare chest.

"*Shh!* What? Oh, that was Elizabeth, Rose. She was just asking me if I wanted another cup of coffee. Do you want to talk to her again? No? Well, then I guess I'll say goodbye now. You'll call my father and tell him we're fine? We'll call him tomorrow morning. How long are we staying in New York? To tell you the truth, I don't know. But we'll call every morning, I promise. Say goodbye to Gloria and Jack and everyone for us, will you? Goodbye, Rose."

Nick leaned over and replaced the telephone receiver, then rolled onto his back and dragged Elizabeth down across his chest. "Come here, wife. I haven't kissed you in at least ten minutes. I think I'm suffering from withdrawal symptoms."

Elizabeth obediently kissed him, then quipped, "I think you might be suffering from guilt, darling. How can you lie so easily? We had take-out pizza for dinner last night, for heaven's sake!"

"Well, you were the one who told your mother we were window-shopping at Tiffany's yesterday," Nick temporized, nibbling on her ear. "Personally, I think we're pretty clever. Nobody suspects a thing."

Elizabeth pushed herself over onto her side and looked around the room. Her canopy bed fit perfectly between two of the dormer windows in the large bedroom, and Nick had already started a fire in the fireplace, which lent a warm golden glow to the rest of the room. She didn't know how he had done it, but somehow Nick had gotten stock boys from Lancaster's to take down her four-poster bed and move it to the house on Prospect Avenue after everyone had left for the wedding. Then those same stock boys had transferred all of Nick's furniture there as well.

Their house on Prospect Avenue. Elizabeth felt a tinge of pleasure run through her as she remembered how she had felt five days earlier after leaving the wedding reception, when Nick had first driven the car into the driveway and parked behind the house. He had called it his wedding present to her, and she had cried on his shoulder as he had carried her across the threshold into the house.

For the last five days they had honeymooned in the house, learning about it and each other, alone together in the world they had made. After all the hustle and bustle of preparing for their wedding, the house was like an island of peace, and Elizabeth was reluctant to ever let the world in again.

Every morning Nick had telephoned either his father or the house on Spring Street, reporting in dutifully and telling whopping fibs about the fun they were having in New York. It was wonderful, a bit silly and just what they needed after months of listening to everyone else tell them what to do.

"How long do you think we can stay here before we have to face everybody?" she asked him now, her bones turning to water as he began nibbling at the side of her throat.

Nick turned her more fully into his arms, his lips a scant inch from hers. "I'm aiming for June, myself."

Elizabeth felt her heart leap. "I love you, Mr. Lancaster," she told him earnestly, raising her hands to encircle his head.

"I think I can live with that, Mrs. Lancaster,"

Nick admitted happily, just before their private world grew even smaller, with room in it for no one but each other.

* * * * *

HARLEQUIN *Super*ROMANCE®

Critically acclaimed author

Tara Taylor Quinn

brings you

The Promise of Christmas

Harlequin Superromance #1309
On sale November 2005

In this deeply emotional story, a woman
unexpectedly becomes the guardian of her
brother's child. Shortly before Christmas,
Leslie Sanderson finds herself coping with
grief, with lingering and fearful memories and
with unforseen motherhood. She also
rediscovers a man from her past who could
help her move toward the promise
of a new future....

Available wherever Harlequin books are sold.

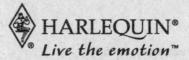

HARLEQUIN®
Live the emotion™

Kate Austin makes
a captivating debut
in this luminous tale
of an unconventional
road trip…and one
woman's metamorphosis.

dragonflies AND **dinosaurs**

KATE AUSTIN

Available December 2005
TheNextNovel.com

HN24

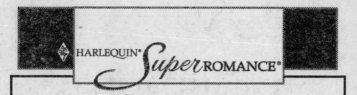

HARLEQUIN *Super*ROMANCE

**A powerful new story from a
RITA® Award-nominated author!**

A Year and a Day
by Inglath Cooper

**Harlequin Superromance #1310
On sale November 2005**

Audrey Colby's life is the envy of most. She's
married to a handsome, successful man, she
has a sweet little boy and they live in a lovely
home in an affluent neighborhood. But
everything is not always as it seems. Only
Nicholas Wakefiled has seen the danger
Audrey's in. Instead of helping, though,
he complicates things even more....

Available wherever Harlequin books are sold.

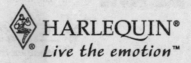

HARLEQUIN®
Live the emotion™